"I love you so much," she whispered, nestling closer to him, content in his warmth and strength.

He bent and kissed her hard on the mouth, arousing the desire within him. But at last he forced himself to let her go. This was a precious gift he had been given, the gift of Lisa's innocent love, and no matter what the personal cost, he must protect it. As long as he could. And that was just it, he thought: How much longer could he pretend?

DOROTHY LEIGH ABEL has an insatiable appetite for life and has expressed many of her own experiences in her novels. Though involved in many activities, from editing the church paper to volunteer work in the local chapter of the American Red Cross, Dorothy feels the most totally alive when she is actively creating a story.

The Whisper Of Love

Dorothy Leigh Abel

HARVEST HOUSE PUBLISHERS
Eugene, Oregon 97402

Other Rhapsody Romance Books:

THE WHISPER OF LOVE

Copyright © 1983 by Dorothy Leigh Abel
Published by Harvest House Publishers
Eugene, Oregon 97402

Second printing, March 1984
ISBN 0-89081-396-5

Printed in the United States of America.

The Whisper
Of Love

Chapter 1✸✸✸✸✸✸✸✸✸✸✸

*T*he rain fell in a downpour. Lisa could barely make out the huge marquee proclaiming Oceanview Shopping Center. She turned her blue Camaro into the empty parking lot and pulled into a space near the drugstore. She climbed out and hurried inside. Selecting a few items from the shelves, she made her way to the rear of the store and the drug counter.

"Hello there, Mr. Hughes."

The elderly pharmacist looked up. "Evening, Miss Palmer. What are you doing out on such a night?"

"I was just on my way home from work. I needed to get a few things in case this storm turns out as bad as they expect."

"Bet there aren't many planes flying tonight."

"We've canceled all flights for the weekend. Our last weather report said this is going to be one of the worst storms Southern California has ever experienced."

"That bad, huh?" the old man said, peering over the edge of his rimless glasses. "You'd better be getting home, young lady."

Lisa nodded her blonde head. "I just wanted to say hi. See you after the storm. I hope."

After paying for her purchases at the front of the store, Lisa ran back to her car. She eased the little Camaro cautiously out of the parking lot and went south on Oceanview Drive. Seeing was difficult in the heavy rain, but the light was green as she approached the nearly deserted intersection and gave a signal to turn left. Traffic was sparse along this residential thoroughfare, so that even while traveling at a slow speed she soon reached Seashore Road. She drove for several miles beside the beach, occasionally taking her eyes from the winding road to glimpse the exasperated sea crashing its noble breakers against the sandy earth.

She passed only a few scattered houses until she turned her car into a flower-lined drive that led to a small cottage of yellow concrete block. She got out and raced through the yard of lofty palms and sturdy yucca plants to a long, narrow porch. The telephone was ringing when she unlocked the front door. Hastily unloading her purse and packages on the coffee table in the living room, she darted down the hall to the bedroom to answer it.

"Lisa?"

"Sue, is that you? This connection is terrible."

"How bad is the storm there?"

"As bad as this connection, and it's getting worse all the time."

"There's a lot of damage in town already. I'm afraid Mark and I won't be able to make it home tonight. Traffic is snarled and—"

"What did you say? I can barely hear you above the cracking and popping."

"We'll be home as soon as we can!" Sue shouted, "But this spoils our plans for the weekend!"

"I guess so."

"We'd better get off the line now. See you, Lisa."

"Bye."

Their plans for the weekend were gone, thought Lisa as she hung up. Sue and Mark were her nearest neighbors, and such good friends, often including her in their plans and introducing her to nice young men. Even if none of them caught her fancy, it was kind of her new friends to try. And she always tried to repay their efforts. They accepted her homemade desserts—her favorite cobblers and pies her mother had taught her to bake—but she could tell they never seemed interested when she talked about what was most important to her—her belief in God.

Yet they did come to church with her occasionally. She frequently invited them and shared her faith in God through His Son. But she sensed that Sue and Mark came to church with her only because they were her friends. They seemed to take only a polite concern in the difference that Jesus had made in her life. Well, she had not been in California long. Sometimes it took years in a Christian's life to bring others to the Lord.

It seemed that everyone had been so kind to Lisa since she had arrived in California. Was it only a year ago that she had left Amarillo with Barbara and driven to the land of her dreams? For as long as she could remember, that golden land had held a special fascination for her—the ocean, the desert, the mountains. After her family's vacation to the southern part of the state when Lisa was 13 she had been totally entranced by all it had to offer. And now to actually live in such a place!

In the small kitchen pantry, Lisa took out several long-stemmed candles and two brass candlesticks. These would do if the electricity went off, she decided, and laid them on the counter by the range, then reached into a paneled cabinet above her head for the matches she kept there. She left to put away her few purchases from the drugstore, and then at the front window in the living room she parted the floral drapes and peeped outside. Biting wind whined through a torrent of rain and blazing lightning darted in jagged fashion about a black sky. Above it all, bellowing thunder approached a deafening peak.

She closed the curtains and turned to survey her cozy little home. "Little" was the exact word to describe it, she thought, although the living room was large enough as it stretched across the front of the cottage. It was done in shades of blue and brown, with a deep blue armchair and matching ottoman positioned near the door. Along the adjacent wall sat two brown couches separated by a cherry hexagon book table with shelves opening on three sides. A lamp of gold ceramic sat on its glossy surface. A matching coffee table sat before the couches. On this long table was a fresh bouquet of poppies and a copy of *Today's Christian Woman.* Beneath her feet lay a thick carpet interwoven in shades of blue and brown.

Lisa stared at the empty wall space across the room. She really had to get something to fill up that area—a television or stereo, perhaps. She didn't care much for TV, but she loved good music and played her portable FM radio all the time when she was home. Well, she would buy a stereo set before too long. It would be her first big purchase from her job earnings.

She went down the short hallway that led from the center of the living room to the back of the cottage. On one side of the hall was a sparkling bathroom done in yellow-and-turquoise decor. Next to it was a small storage-and-utility room containing a washer and dryer and an ancient freezer. Across the hall was a modest bedroom with a row of closets occupying one wall. Lisa came out of the hallway into the modern green-and-yellow kitchen extending across the back of the cottage. It was supplied with all the latest electrical equipment. A round table and chairs sat near sliding glass doors that opened onto a generous patio overlooking the beach.

Lisa sliced a ham sandwich and poured a glass of milk from the refrigerator. She was still eating at the round table by the door when a shattering bolt of lightning struck somewhere

near the house. She jumped. Seconds later the lights went
out. She rose and went to the counter by the range, lighting
the candles she had left there. Back at the table, she wondered
how long the storm would last as she downed the last bites
of her sandwich and finished her milk. Much damage was
taking place outside, but she felt secure in her snug little
home as long as the wind didn't grow too wild, she decided,
offering a silent prayer that it would not.

Lisa took off her shoes and settled on the couch in the living room with the candles nearby on the book table, and tried
to get absorbed in a new novel she had bought at the drugstore on her way home from work. But the light was poor,
and she soon gave it up and blew out the candles, deciding
to take a short nap. Perhaps the storm would be over when
she woke.

It was eight o'clock when Lisa roused and lit the candles
again, glancing at her watch on the table. The thunder and
lightning hadn't stopped, she noticed, and the wind still blew
furiously, whipping the turbulent rainfall relentlessly about
the house and slapping the unruly tide disobediently against
the sand. She got up and wandered down the hall to the kitchen, pausing at the sliding door to peek out between the
vertical blinds. In a flash of lightning that tore across the sky,
she glimpsed a deserted beach, an angry, snarling sea, and—

What was that?

A solid movement in the water caught her eye. It was too
small an object to be a boat—a part of one maybe, she decided, and stood watching a moment longer. Whatever it was
seemed to have some life of its own.

Quickly Lisa rolled the sliding door open and stepped outside. On the patio she lost sight of whatever it was in the
darkness. But in a moment she heard a voice call out. Someone was calling for help!

Lisa sprang from the patio and raced across the lawn down
to the beach with the wind and rain flapping her thin dress

tightly about her long, slender figure. In a blaze of lightning that illuminated the sky she could barely make out a figure, approximately 50 yards offshore, thrashing helplessly in the choppy water. She waded out and began to swim, the towering waves lashing her cruelly back and forth.

"It's all right! I've come to help you!" she cried when finally she reached the frantic figure.

The man didn't seem to understand and continued to fling himself about in his battle with the sea. Lisa tried to grab him, but he knocked her away as he fought desperately for what was left of his life.

"You have to stop fighting and let me help you!" she shouted.

Without warning the man fell back in the water, completely submerging himself. Lisa reached for his sinking body, pulling his head and shoulders out of the ocean, but he began flailing his arms wildly again, restricting her rescue attempt. Once more she tried to reason with him, but it became obvious by the violent conflict he waged that he was too far gone to comprehend. Weary of the inane struggle, she grabbed at the panic-stricken man and slapped him hard across the face, trying to bring him to his senses before he drowned them both.

Instantly the tension left his frenzied body. She put her left arm under his chin to hold his head out of the water and started to make her way to shore. But the waves surged over them, causing her to lose her grip. He began floating away. Groping about in the darkness, she spotted him a few yards away and swam to his side. Getting a better hold, she continued toward the beach, with the powerful force of the wind throwing the giant rollers in her face. Lisa forged on, but the destructive sea was too demanding and she lost her hold on him once more.

"Oh, please, God!" she cried out in utter desperation. "We need Your help! We can't make it on our own!"

She swam over to the man and secured her arm across his chest this time. Then slowly they made their way to the beach, the wind and rain growing calmer, as though allowing them a break from the long battle they waged.

Safely out of the water at last, Lisa dragged the man up to the patio, bent over him, and laid her head on his chest. He wasn't breathing. She put her hand in his mouth and found no foreign objects, so she tilted his head back and covered his nostrils with her thumb and forefinger. Then she opened his mouth wide and placed hers over it. Rhythmically she blew her breath into his lungs, until in a short time he began shallow breathing. She maintained this mouth-to-mouth resuscitation until his breathing was smooth and regular.

When some of her energy had returned, Lisa dragged the man's powerless body into the house. Once they were inside, the storm seemed to resume as quickly and with as much force as it had before.

❋   ❋   ❋

The six-foot frame of Brian Sommervale lay sprawled on the kitchen floor. Shining black hair framed his deeply tanned face with its high, prominent cheekbones and long, straight nose. Limp eyelids lay closed over his dark brown eyes and tattered clothes clung to his lean, hard-muscled body.

Lisa left him and went to the living room for the candles. She put them on the table by the door and leaned over to look at her nearly-drowned victim. Staring in disbelief, she excitedly realized who he was and knelt down beside him in dazed wonder at what this well-known man was doing out in the ocean, all alone, fighting for his life. She regarded his handsome bronze face, remembering the wonderful things she had heard about him and thinking how he surely didn't look at that particular moment like the pillar of excellence who had taken the world's problems for his own. She would have smiled at the sight of this forceful, compassionate, humorous man, posed in weakness and in need of help himself, were it not for the seriousness of his situation. He was unconscious, or nearly so.

She touched his damp forehead. It was cold. She felt his strong, brown hands. They were like ice. She rose and hurried into the bathroom, taking several fluffy towels from the linen closet. At the door of the bedroom she paused. She had to get him out of his torn, soaked clothes, but what could she put on him? Terry's pajamas! She used to sleep in her brother's pajamas when she was a teenager. They were so big and comfortable. And her mother had sent them along, sentimentally, with the box of household items she had mailed to her daughter following that very calm, very assured phone call that Lisa had made to her parents—announcing that she wouldn't be coming home at the end of her vacation last summer, that she wouldn't be returning to her third year of college in the fall.

How thankful she was for the trust and understanding of her family, for the foundation of Christian love they had laid down for her! She reminisced about the rambling white frame house where she had grown up, of the big porch where endless happy hours (between school and chores) had been wiled away in the bright red swing with one board missing way in the back. How secure her life had been in that casual suburban setting! Although they had not had an abundance of material possessions, her father, a hard working man all his life, had given his family the best he could provide. And more importantly, he had brought up his children in a God-fearing home. They had been faithful to their church attendance and had carried home the values taught there, applying them to their daily lives. Christ was still the head of the Palmer household, including Lisa.

Her parents hadn't wanted her to move so far away from home, but they had been willing to let her go because they thought she was ready. Well, she certainly wasn't ready for anything like this!

Back in the kitchen, Lisa dried Brian Sommervale's face and hair with one of the towels, then nudged him gently onto his side to remove what was left of his torn shirt. After drying the top half of his body with another towel, she put Terry's pajama shirt on him and began undoing his trousers.

"Oh, my goodness!" she exclaimed aloud. "How am I ever going to manage this?"

With a small giggle, she closed her eyes and clumsily pulled off his ragged trousers, and then tugged on the pajama pants. Thankful when she had finally completed that task, she took the candles and left to turn down the covers on her bed. After she dragged Brian Sommervale down the short hall to her room, she stood in the middle of the floor considering how she would get him into bed.

Gathering the little strength she could still muster, Lisa pulled him over to the bed, then reached down and lifted the top of his languid body, placing his arms and head on the bed. Holding him that way with one hand, she raised first one muscular leg and then the other till all of him was positioned on the edge of the bed. When she let go he promptly rolled onto the floor. Suppressing an urge to laugh, she tried again. When he started rolling a second time, she teamed all her resources and lunged forcefully on top of him, flattening him out completely. Breathlessly she got up and went around to the other side and tugged him over to the center. Satisfied that he wouldn't roll out again, she covered him with the soft blanket already on the bed and went to the closet to get another. He was probably in shock from being so long in the icy water, she decided, and would have to be kept warm until she could get a doctor to see him.

After Lisa covered her "guest" with the second blanket, she reached in haste for the telephone on the night table, while opening the drawer for the telephone directory. Sue and Mark's doctor was good—she had seen him for an ear infection shortly after coming to California. If she could only get him to come out in this storm! Oh, but of course he would when he learned that his patient was Brian Sommervale.

So wrapped in her thoughts was Lisa that for an instant the silence in her ear didn't register in her mind. The phone was dead! But what did she expect in such adverse weather conditions? Reluctantly she replaced the receiver and returned the directory to the drawer. What should she do now?

Perhaps she could go to the doctor's home. But a peek out the window in the bedroom told her that such an attempt might invite serious harm to herself. And then how would Brian Sommervale do here by himself?

Lisa pulled a deep armchair from across the room and placed it by the bed. When she collapsed into its comfortable depths, she found her mind too filled with concern to give way to the needs of her exhausted body. What would she do if her famous "guest" didn't come out of his stupor? What if he just lay there in her bed until he died? And she couldn't even get to a doctor!

A sickening wave of horror spread over her, and for one frightening second she visualized Brian Sommervale lying cold and sallow, never again to grace the world with his Christian love and generosity. He couldn't die. He simply couldn't. Maybe she couldn't call a doctor, but she didn't need a telephone to call on Someone else.

Lord, she prayed in her heart, *You helped us through the worst of this ordeal—please don't take him home yet. The world still needs him so.*

Lisa rose from the chair and leaned over the bed to get a better view of her hapless intruder. He was a sleeping Apollo, she thought, with his high, prominent cheekbones, straight nose, and full, soft mouth. She remembered his familiar, well-loved smile, slightly crooked and so sweet and compelling. How a man such as he had managed to escape marriage in his 30 years she couldn't understand. And as if it weren't enough that he was such an attractive man, there was his unique reputation—his tenderness and sensitivity toward people in need.

Lisa crossed the room to the dresser to examine her tall reflection in the mirror. She was a soaked disaster from head to toe and her blonde hair was a mass of tangles. She chose a long robe from the closet, took one of the candles, and went into the bathroom to change. Then she collected the wet towels and Brian Sommervale's battered clothes, which she hung over the shower-curtain rod.

In the bedroom she checked her charge again and sank wearily into the comfortable chair beside the bed. Soon she gave way to drowsiness in spite of the thoughts speeding like a galloping stallion through her mind.

The next morning Lisa was awakened by slight moaning sounds coming from the bed. Brian Sommervale had begun to move about in his semiconscious state. She tucked the edges of the covers securely under each side of the mattress, giving him a firmer anchor lest he should roll too far, and stayed by his side till he was resting peacefully again.

The storm had ended sometime during the night, leaving the world around them in a crippling shambles. Trees had been uprooted and lay at myriad angles across entangled streets. Power lines were torn down and left hanging in a menace about the city—and the telephone was still dead. Brightly colored lawn furniture floated in the ocean like disordered toys left carelessly behind by some capricious giant after a day of play. And usually sturdy trash cans, their rancid contents in an upheaval, streamed out in disarray along streets and beaches.

Amid the damage and confusion, Lisa began to think of some way to feed her "patient," as her eminent guest had quite obviously become, for she knew that even in his senseless condition he had to have nourishment, especially

after the struggle he had carried on for his life the night
before. In the utility room she kept a two-burner camping
stove and a can of gas, and in the pantry she surveyed rows
of canned goods—enough to suffice any appetite. She selected
a can of beef broth and heated it on the little stove, but her
famous patient was reluctant to eat, rousing only enough to
sip the warm liquid she offered. She fed him diligently at
varying intervals throughout the day, and when nightfall
came and he was still resting comfortably, she resumed her
sleeping arrangement of the night before, dozing uneasily in
the chair beside the bed.

Caught unaware by a noise during the early morning hours,
Lisa leaped from the chair in barely enough time to keep her
patient from bounding out of bed. She flung herself boldly
on top of his distorted figure, shoving him back to the middle. He groaned and talked erratically while trying to free
himself from the warm retreat she had made, and at one point
her trifling weight was no match even for his impaired
strength, for he pushed her aside, lunging forward like a
winged creature about to take flight. Using her body as a
lever, Lisa forced him back under the covers and held him
there with trembling hands.

When at last he grew calm she felt his brow. He was burn-
ing with fever. She lit a candle and dashed into the bathroom,
grabbing rubbing alcohol and aspirin from the medicine
cabinet. From the linen closet she took some washcloths, and
in the kitchen got a plastic cup, then crushed the aspirin and
mixed it with some leftover broth. Back in the bedroom, she
sank down on the edge of the bed and cradled his sweltering
head in the crook of her arm as she fed him the mixture. Some
of the liquid spilled onto Terry's pajamas, but she kept coax-
ing until he had drunk most of it.

Throughout the night Brian Sommervale tossed and raged.
Lisa gave him aspirin and bathed his face and arms with
washcloths drenched in alcohol. When morning finally

dawned the fever had broken and once more he slept quietly.

Despondency hung like an ominous cloud over Lisa the entire day. Even with his fever gone a desolate kind of fear gnawed at her. She knew nothing about caring for a person in his condition. What if he got pneumonia? Or what if he really did die? She had no way of getting medical or any other kind of help. The nearest house, if she could get to it, belonged to Sue and Mark, and it was a half-mile away. And anyway, they weren't home. The burden of responsibility so unexpectedly thrust upon her weighed heavily on Lisa's shoulders, and her every breath that day was a silent prayer that God would help her take proper care of this special man.

That night she hovered at his bedside like a first-time mother with her long-awaited newborn babe. If he so much as drew a deep breath, she was there immediately to attend to him.

The third morning after the storm, Lisa slept soundly in the chair by the bed, totally exhausted from her harrowing experience.

Chapter 2 ✹✹✹✹✹✹✹✹✹✹✹✹

*B*rian scanned the room of contemporary fur-
nishings. Beneath the window to his left sat a small oak chest.
A photograph of a family grouping in a silver frame rested
at an angle on top. Across the room a row of closets filled
the wall, with one door slightly ajar, revealing an array of
feminine clothing in different colors and fabrics. Along the
adjacent wall, near the door, stood an oak dresser. A white
Bible and a bouquet of bright poppies occupied its surface.
Two very short candles in their brass candlesticks stood
nearby.

His eyes came to rest on the lovely crumpled mass in the
armchair beside the bed. He gazed at her long, slender body
clothed in pale blue pajamas and flowing robe. Several curling locks of shoulder-length blonde hair lay in a becoming
arrangement of tangles around her face. He studied her for
a long time. She was one of classic, almost perfect beauty,
with high cheekbones, small nose, and wide, even mouth.
Her fine, creamy complexion had a tawny glow, acquired
from just the right amount of time in the sun.

Brian regarded the beautiful young woman in silence for
a few more minutes while he tried to sort out his thoughts.
But his memory was incomplete. He could recall only bits
and pieces of the boat ride, the sudden storm, the yelling and
running around. Then fathoms and fathoms of icy water from

which there seemed no retreat. Then warm hands and reassuring words. Then...

He didn't know. He couldn't remember.

His thoughts returned to the present, and he wondered how he came to be in what was probably the lovely lady's bed and how much she had had to do with it. He tried to get up, but fell back in weakness, resting his head against the soft pillow that had been his staunch ally during many dubious hours prior to his awakening. Satisfied that he was all in one piece and not in any dire pain, he decided to try to rouse the young lady asleep at his bedside.

"Good morning!" he said in his soft, clear baritone. When she didn't stir he spoke again.

Lisa opened her eyes and blinked. She gave him a wide and somewhat awkward smile. "Good morning. How are you feeling?"

"Fine—I think. But I'm a little weak."

"You've been through quite an ordeal," she said, feeling slightly strange in his presence now that he was fully roused.

"How did I get here?"

"I saw you out in the water. Then I heard you call out. Don't you remember?"

Brian ran one hand thoughtfully through his shining black hair as he tried to remember more about the past Friday evening. "I was out on a boat with some friends when word came over the shortwave that a severe storm was about to hit. We tried to get back, but it came down on us too fast. There was a lot of confusion, and before anyone knew it we had capsized."

"What happened then?" she asked in her soft Southern drawl.

"I'm not sure. I swam around for awhile. Then somehow I got separated from everyone."

Lisa began telling him about their unusual weekend, and

when she finished he lay staring blankly at her. "You saved my life, young lady."

"You weren't too far from the beach—you probably would've made it on your own," she said, trying to convince herself as well as him.

"No, I was just about gone." He rubbed the side of his face. "Now I know why my jaw is so sore. You must have really let me have it out there!"

"I'm so sorry. I didn't mean to hurt you, but I had to do something. I was afraid you were going to drown us both."

"I'm glad you did." He gazed at her, admiration clear in his dark eyes. "And you managed all this on your own?"

"No, I had some outside help, I think. Mr. Sommervale—"

"You know who I am?"

"Yes, but I didn't recognize you at first. It was so dark, and with all the confusion I didn't pay any attention. Then when I got you in the house and took a good look, there you were. I knew you right away even without those super-looking glasses you wear."

Brian glanced down at the yellow striped pajamas he was wearing. Then he tossed his head back and filled the room with his wonderful, rich laughter. "There I was in all my glory!"

"Oh, no, Mr. Sommervale—" She stopped, blushing beneath her sunny glow, and Brian Sommervale howled till his broad shoulders shook furiously. Lisa watched him, listening to the blissful sound of his laughter. It seemed to begin somewhere way down in his soul and grow and grow till it burst forth from his throat in glorious, boundless freedom. She had never heard anyone laugh quite the way he did. It seemed to consume every part of him and all at the same time. Even his eyes laughed, twinkling, glinting at her from where he lay on the bed.

"I know I've been a lot of trouble," he said when finally he could speak again.

"No, I was glad to do anything I could. But you had me pretty scared for awhile. I thought you were getting pneumonia when you became so feverish and went so wild. And I couldn't call a doctor—"

"I'm like that most of the time," he injected jovially.

They both laughed then, and Lisa gazed with sweet fondness at him. How easy it was to talk to this man who was a stranger to her even though his name and reputation were household words in many places!

"Tell me about this outside help you had saving my life," he said.

"It was the Lord, Mr. Sommervale." She told him how the storm had suddenly quieted in the middle of her struggle to get him to shore. "I know the Lord helped me, because the storm began again as soon as we got inside."

"I like the way you say, 'The *Lord* helped me.' You sound as though you know Him personally."

"Yes, I've been a Christian since I was ten. My parents introduced me to Him very early in my life."

Brian Sommervale smiled his crooked smile and nodded his dark head approvingly. "Say, you have me at a disadvantage, you know. You drag me out of the ocean, put me in your bed, then sit up with me night and day, feeding me soup and listening to my insane ramblings—all this and I don't even know your name."

She smiled fondly at him again. "I'm sorry. I should have told you before. My name is Lisa Palmer."

"Lisa Palmer," he repeated, savoring the name on the tip of his tongue and gazing levelly at her. "Young lady, you're about the loveliest sight these eyes have ever seen."

Lisa ran a graceful hand over her tousled hair. "Thank you, but I must be a sight right now."

"What a sight!" he said, easing himself into an upright position.

She jumped up. "Here, Mr. Sommervale, let me help you."

She picked up the pillows, fluffing them with care behind his back.

Brian looked at her long, slim body, smiling with typical male approval. Then he patted the bed beside him. "Sit down a minute." When she hesitated, he smiled again. "Please."

She sat down abruptly. How could she say no to that smile? It was utter charisma.

"I'm deeply indebted to you," he began. "If it weren't for you I'd still be out in the Pacific Ocean somewhere—water-logged. I owe you my life, and there isn't any way I can ever repay you for all you've done."

"Please, Mr. Sommervale, I know you're grateful, but you don't have to thank me."

"Wait," he said, touching a gentle finger to her lips. "I haven't finished yet. You saved my life without any thought to your own risk, and I'll never forget it." The magnetic grin spread over his face. "It's just a good thing for you we aren't in China. They have an old custom over there that says if one person saves another person's life, that life belongs to him, or her, until death." He ran his tongue along the edges of his perfect white teeth. "So you see, you're very fortunate. You only have to put up with my gratitude, but you could have been stuck with all of me."

She gave a small laugh, thinking how many hearts would probably flutter at the possibility of such an arrangement. But it didn't occur to her to include her own among them.

"Now if there's anything at all I can do for you," Brian Sommervale continued.

"There isn't anything you can do for me. You don't even have to thank me. You bring about so many good things, you help so many people who can't help themselves. Just don't ever stop doing these things, and that will be all the thanks I'll ever need."

"I won't. I promise."

A little embarrassed at her frankness, Lisa rose and went back to her chair.

"How bad was the storm?" he asked, sensing her self-consciousness and bringing up a new subject.

"It was the worst storm I've ever experienced. We don't have any electricity and the phone's out."

"Where are we, anyway?"

"Oceanview."

He glanced around. "This is a nice place you have."

"Thank you. But it really isn't mine. I was fortunate to be able to rent it," she said, and launched into a brief account of coming to California on vacation at the end of her second year of college. "My friend Barb went back home to finish school, but I couldn't leave. I love the beach most of all, but there are also the mountains and the desert. I guess I'm hooked now, like so many other people. I don't even mind the smog. Well, not too much."

Brian gave Lisa a lopsided grin, his brown eyes glinting at her with warmth and amusement.

"Barb and I went to that little church over on Harmony Beach Drive while we were here on vacation," she continued. "I met Mr. and Mrs. Larson at church. They're the sweetest old couple. They own this cottage—it was their first home when they came to California years ago. They couldn't bear to part with it after they had prospered and built a big new home, so they keep it and rent it very reasonably. It means more to them to have someone living here who will take care of it than to get a large rental amount for it."

Brian flicked a glance to the night clothes he wore. "Are these your husband's pajamas?"

Lisa flushed and laughed at the same time, remembering the ordeal of trying to dress and undress him and keep a modicum of modesty too. "I'm not married, Mr. Sommervale. Those are my brother's pajamas. I used to like to wear them when we were teenagers. I still wear them sometimes."

He smiled and said, "What do you do when you're not rescuing and nursing a near-drowning victim?"

"I'm a secretary for Southern Pacific Airways. I handle the reservations and do all the paperwork. And I try to get in as much flying time as possible."

"You're a pilot too?"

"Yes, but I just have my private license. I love flying. I used to beg my Uncle Lamarr to take me up. He flew during World War Two and afterward he kept it up. He has a little Piper I dearly love. When I was older he taught me a lot about flying. Then during the summer after I graduated from high school I worked part-time to get the money to take flying lessons so I could get my private license."

"It's exciting being in the sky, isn't it?"

"Yes. Looking down on the world is a thrill I can't describe, but it's more than that. It's a whole different world up there. I've seen sights that only God and I know about. I guess it's a very serene feeling. Sometimes I go up just to get away from everyday things. In the sky I can really come to terms with myself and with life. It seems like everything falls into its proper perspective up there."

"I know just what you mean," Brian said, and flashed his dark brown gaze toward the photograph sitting on the oak chest nearby. "Is that your family over there?"

Lisa nodded. "That's Mom and Dad and the three of us kids," she said in her low drawl. "My brother's in college and my sister's in her last year of high school." She paused as a sudden melancholy feeling washed over her. "I miss my family, but Sue and Mark have been just great."

"And who are Sue and Mark?" he inquired in a kind, thoughtful tone.

"They're a young married couple who live down the beach. They stayed in town because the storm was too bad for them to get home. Mark is a CPA for Bratten Industries. Sue is a legal secretary for the legal office of Penwell and Stoller. They have introduced me to a lot of nice people, but most of their friends are married couples." She paused briefly to brush a lock of blonde hair away from her forehead. "I go with them sometimes on weekends when they take their motorcycles into the desert. Mark loves that." She stopped again. What was wrong with her? She had been prattling on as if this man cared about all the insignificant details of her life. But he was so easy to talk to! "Oh, Mr. Sommervale, I'm sorry. I didn't mean to talk and talk." She sprang to her feet. "I know you must be famished after all you've been through. I'll go fix you something besides broth."

Amused at her chatter, Brian gave a hint of his famous smile. "Will you do something else first?"

She stared at him. "Yes. What is it?"

"Will you please stop calling me 'Mr. Sommervale'? That's quite a mouthful. Just call me Brian."

Lisa's eyes were fastened on him in utter amazement. Did she realize just who she had been so leisurely conversing with? This man was a wealthy philanthropist, traveling thousands of miles each year to help people in need. And yet he was as friendly and casual as your next-door neighbor. She had heard so much about this highly-regarded Christian man, but had never dreamed of being a witness to any of the things that had earned him his well-deserved reputation.

"All right...Brian." She said it almost reverently. "And please call me Lisa."

"I'm sure getting hungry, Lisa," he said with his beautiful, lopsided grin.

Lisa stared at him in unbelief for another few seconds, then went out to the kitchen and began rummaging through the canned goods in the pantry. Soon she asked, "How would you like pork 'n beans, new potatoes, Vienna sausage, and some hot coffee?"

"Sounds delicious."

While Lisa prepared "breakfast," Brian tried sitting on the

edge of the bed. He was weaker than he thought, however, and his dark head reeled as he swung his legs onto the thick carpet. He slid back between the covers, choosing to wait until he had eaten before trying to get up.

When Lisa returned she had changed into jeans and shirt, and Brian admired the graceful carriage of her slim, curving body as she came toward him with a tray of food. She placed it on his lap as he said, "Where's yours?"

"In the kitchen."

"Since I can't make it in there just yet, why don't you eat in here with me?"

This man was unbelievable! "Well, sure if you want me to."

Lisa returned in a minute with a tray for herself, balancing it on her lap in the chair beside the bed while they closed their eyes in the prayer of thanks he offered. They chatted comfortably while they ate.

"Are you planning to go back to college one of these days?" he asked.

"Yes. I'm not even sure why I quit. I suppose I really don't know what career I want to pursue. I love my job at Southern Pacific. I'll probably stay as long as they want me. Maybe I'll finish school at night."

Later, when their hunger had been satisfied, Lisa took their trays back to the kitchen while Brian practiced getting up. She returned shortly to find him sitting uncertainly on the edge of the bed.

"It sure is surprising what a boat ride and a little fall in the water can do to a person!" he observed lightly.

"You'd better take it easy for awhile," she responded, sounding like a mother hen. "You're bound to have lost a lot of strength."

But soon Brian felt better, and it wasn't long until he was walking around the room with a certain amount of grace.

From the back of her closet Lisa produced a pair of faded jeans and a paint-stained T-shirt. "These belonged to my brother too. I use the shirt to clean house in and work in the yard. I don't wear the jeans anymore. They're too big, but I used to take them in at the waist and wear them when we were teenagers. I hate to offer you such old clothes," she added apologetically, "but it's all I have, and I know you'd like to get out of those pajamas."

Brian accepted the clothing with his typical charm and good humor. "No shoes to go with them?"

"I'm afraid not," she laughed.

By early evening Brian had ventured out to the patio. It was a warm, slightly overcast evening in early May. A soft breeze stirred and a gently rippling surf swept across the shore. Brian was sitting in a comfortable lounger glancing through a three-day-old newspaper when Lisa burst joyfully out the kitchen door.

"The electricity's back on!"

He looked up. "That's great. Now if I could just read the print in this paper a little better."

"Well, as soon as the water gets hot you can take a bath. How's that?"

"Not me. I've had enough water to last a lifetime," he said, a joking tone behind his crooked smile.

"Don't be silly. You'll feel better when you're cleaned up."

"If you say so, but you go first."

"Are you being a gentleman or do I really look so bad I need to go first?"

"You look just awful," he teased. "Don't even wait for the water to heat."

They laughed affectionately at each other, and Lisa felt suddenly as if she had known Brian Sommervale all her life. "I love the way you laugh," she said impulsively. "It's so beautiful and invigorating. And do you know you have the most wonderful smile?"

"If you think all that flattery will make up for the messy way you look," he said, "you're right."

They laughed again and then Lisa turned and went back into the house.

After their evening meal, Lisa cleaned up the spoiled food in the refrigerator, thankful all the while for the food which was still good in the old freezer in the utility room. That night they sat in the living room listening to the account of the storm on her FM radio. They learned that some areas were still without electricity, and that it would be another day before the roads were cleared of debris enough for driving. And it would be longer, according to the report, before telephone service would be restored.

The newscast concluded with an account of Brian's mishap:

> A number of injuries have been reported, but as yet no casualties in the severe storm of this weekend. One note, however. Multimillionaire philanthropist Brian Sommervale, who resides at an estate on the coast in Brenthall, has been missing since the yacht on which he was sailing capsized at approximately 6:30 Friday evening. Reports from the Coast Guard indicate that all other persons aboard were brought to safety. The yacht overturned within a half-mile of Oceanview, making it possible for another boater to have picked up the world-famous humanitarian. A spokesman for the Coast Guard said that pending no further developments, a search for the millionaire's body will begin first thing tomorrow morning.

Lisa looked over at her renowned guest, wondering what thoughts were going on behind the striking features of his bronze face. Brian's rich baritone broke in on her musings.

"I need to get home as soon as possible."

"I'll be happy to lend you my car, but do you think you should try tonight? According to the report the roads are still pretty blocked with fallen trees and power lines."

"I'll wait till morning. But you'll have to drive. I don't see well enough without my glasses."

"I just wish there were some way to get in touch with your family."

He shook his head. "What they must be going through right now!"

Later, after a brief, good-natured battle over their sleeping arrangements, Brian insisted that Lisa reclaim her bedroom while he took extra covers to the couch.

"I hope you won't feel uncomfortable tonight," he said, "with a strange man sleeping on your couch."

A strange man? Brian Sommervale? Absurd! He seemed as familiar to her as a brother. Well, almost. And anyway, he was a brother. A brother in Christ!

Chapter 3 ✳✳✳✳✳✳✳✳✳✳✳✳

*L*isa pulled in the driveway and parked her car behind Mark's black TransAm. She got out and hurried to the house where her friends were on the patio having lunch. Sue was shorter than Lisa, with lively gray eyes and a pretty girlish face. Her husband was a wide, solidly built man, not as tall as Brian Sommervale, and his hair and eyes were the color of toasted almonds.

"Have you been home long?" Lisa called as she crossed the yard to where they sat at a wooden table overlooking the calm sea.

"Not long," Sue answered. "We went by the store because we knew everything would be spoiled in the fridge."

"You want some lunch?" Mark asked as Lisa joined them at the table.

"In a minute, but first I have something to tell you that you won't believe."

Lisa began telling them about the past weekend, being careful not to omit even the most insignificant detail. They listened in stunned silence, an occasional expression of surprise and uncertainty crossing their already-startled faces. Lisa wound up her incredible story with particulars of the morning's activities.

"Brian's family and friends are totally unlike my concept of wealthy people," she said. "His parents are visiting from

San Francisco, and they're so warm and gracious. The place was full of people when I drove him home. They were waiting to hear from the Coast Guard, half out of the minds with fear that he'd been washed up on the beach somewhere."

"And if it hadn't been for you, he would have," Sue interjected.

"Well, thank God somebody was around when he needed help."

"Who else did you meet at his estate?" asked Sue.

"I met so many people, but his secretary, Maude, seemed really nice. And Livy, Brian's cook. She's a treat. Everyone seemed like one big happy family—the servants, the friends, everyone."

"Did you meet his sister?" Mark asked.

"No, she wasn't there."

"I've heard she's kind of wild."

"Wild" was an accurate description of the car that had whizzed recklessly past Lisa as she was leaving Brian's estate. It was going so fast that she couldn't tell who was driving, but from her fleeting glimpse a young woman had appeared to be at the wheel.

"We've driven past Brian Sommervale's estate," said Sue. "It's beautiful. But you can't see his mansion from the road. What's it like?"

"Absolutely glorious. The whole place is breathtaking. And Brian is—"

"What's all this Brian stuff?" Sue broke in with a curious gleam in her gray eyes. "Come on, now, are you sure you told us *everything* about the weekend you two spent together?"

"Oh, Sue! It's just that Brian's such a friendly person. He isn't at all pretentious. If you didn't already know who he was, you certainly wouldn't guess by the way he acts. He's so natural and unassuming."

"What does he have to say about what happened?" Mark inquired.

"He's very grateful. He just went on about how he'd be dead if it weren't for me, and how much he appreciated all I'd done."

"Just imagine, saving the life of a millionaire, and the benevolent Brian Sommervale at that!" Sue announced. "I bet he'll give you an enormous reward."

"I already have that straight with him. I told him I didn't want anything, and I don't think he'll offer, knowing how I feel."

"Yes, but you know how he is, going around giving his money to one needy cause or another," Mark said.

"They say he's a real nut about things like that," added Sue.

"I'm not a needy cause," Lisa drawled.

"No, but you did do a couple of things for him," Sue said, "like pulling him out of the ocean when he was about to go under for the last time and sitting up with him while he was delirious with fever. People don't do things like that every day."

"Boats don't capsize every day either," Lisa responded. "Anyway, even if he offered me something, I wouldn't take it."

"You've got rocks for brains, Lisa!" Mark blazed. "If he wants to show his appreciation, let him. He's a millionaire! He can afford to give you anything."

"Sure," Sue agreed. "Take whatever he offers. You're just a working girl living on a budget like everyone else."

"Maybe someone else would jump at the chance to take money or something from Brian, but I'm not about to. Somehow, after meeting him, it just doesn't seem right. You can't imagine how sweet and kind he is, and I just couldn't accept money from him."

It was on the tip of Lisa's tongue to tell her friends about Brian's parting gesture when he had walked her out to her car as she was leaving his estate that morning. But something inside kept her from speaking. Although she knew that Brian must treat everyone with the same kindness, still his good-bye had been special and meant only for her. And she sensed it wasn't just because she had rescued him.

She had seen a different Brian when they first arrived at his home. After the devoted reception he gave and received from his family and friends, he had changed rapidly from the casual to the composed. But it was necessary, Lisa had decided, to conduct business of the magnitude that he did. And even though he kept his business simple in terms of staff, a person would have to possess profound discipline and devotion to meet the relentless demands that came to him from nearly everywhere.

It was Brian's devotion that had touched her so when they said good-bye.

"I'll have to give a story to the media," he had said. "Are you aware of what this will involve?"

"I hadn't given it any thought."

"When I tell the world you saved my life, you'll become the attraction of the hour," he had said. "Everyone will want to see the woman who pulled Brian Sommervale out of the Pacific Ocean."

"Surely you're exaggerating. Anyway, it's *your* story."

"Without you the story would be an obituary."

That was when he had given her the tiny slip of paper. "This is my private phone number," he had explained. "If you ever need me for anything, I'll be at this number. When I'm gone, someone here will tell you how to get in touch with me."

"Thank you, Brian. Thank you very much," Lisa had said after recovering from her surprise.

He had gazed tenderly into her eyes and reached for her hand. "Thank you again for saving my life. You know I can't adequately express that kind of gratitude in mere words.

Maybe I can't express it in any way, but if you ever need me for any reason, just reach out and I'll be there." He had leaned over then and touched her cheek with a soft kiss.

Over a cottage-cheese-and-peach salad with iced tea, Lisa chatted leisurely with her friends about their experiences of the past three days. Sue and Mark related what they considered a rather commonplace tale compared with Lisa's: auto accidents and traffic tie-ups on the wet streets as they had slowly made their way to a friend's apartment in town; getting drenched in a mad dash from the car to the apartment building; and sharing a meager and cold supply of canned goods and leftovers with three other people.

"Have you called your parents?" Sue asked at the conclusion of their weekend story.

Lisa looked dumbfounded. "With all that's happened, I hadn't even thought about it! I'd better call them as soon as I get home."

That evening after dinner Lisa was listening to the news broadcast on her radio when the account of Brian's rescue was given. Her telephone was ringing before she even had time to digest the report.

"Oh, Lisa!" Sue exclaimed, "You'll be famous! I just heard Brian Sommervale's story on TV."

"I'm afraid he exaggerated the whole thing," Lisa said. "He made it sound like I—"

"I think he was just trying to emphasize how much you helped him," Sue broke in. "But what difference does it make? The point is that Brian Sommervale would be dead right now if it weren't for you! I'll bet half the reporters in L.A. will be after you for a complete story."

Wednesday morning life in and around the Los Angeles area was back to normal. Everywhere people were getting into their cars and heading for the freeways, bound for their jobs. Lisa joined the throng and drove to Southern Pacific Airways, a small regional airline located at Wesley Field, a privately owned airstrip not far from Oceanview. The airline, owned jointly by two brothers, catered to the elite class of Southern California.

The office, situated at one end of the field, wasn't far from the two hangars where Vic and Jerry Manning kept their three planes ready for flight. Vic, the younger of the two brothers, took care of the maintenance, and Jerry did the flying. Other than their secretary, they had one more employee, a pilot named Carl Hampton.

Lisa parked her car in front of the low, rectangular building that served as an office. Inside the concrete building, a formica counter ran the width of the room, separating the waiting area from the office. Several cushioned chairs and a long wooden bench lined the walls of the waiting room. Behind the counter sat a broad pine desk and a metal filing cabinet. Beyond the office, to the rear of the structure, was a restroom and a small kitchen with a door that led out to the hangars.

A man of medium height and curly brown hair looked up from the desk as Lisa came in. "What do you say, kid?"

"Morning, Vic."

"Had quite a weekend, didn't you?" he said with a grinning face.

Jerry Manning came in the door behind Lisa. He was slightly taller than his brother, but had the same lean build and dark wavy hair. "Why, it's our intrepid little heroine," he said to his secretary.

She turned, smiling at him.

"That was a terrific thing you did," Jerry said, quite serious now.

"It sure was, kid," Vic agreed. He got up and crossed the room with a steaming mug of coffee in his hand.

"I sure wouldn't want to go through something like that again," Lisa replied. "But I'm thankful everything turned out all right." She started for the desk.

"What you did will probably get a lot of publicity around here," Vic said.

"Oh, I hope not."

"What's wrong with publicity?" Jerry asked with his customary concern for their livelihood.

"I just don't see any need for a lot of fuss."

"It's a good human interest story," Jerry said. "When you give out interviews, be sure and say you work for Southern Pacific."

A wide grin on her face, Lisa said, *"If* I give any, I'll see that Southern Pacific gets mentioned." She took a seat at her desk. "What's up for today?"

"I've got a flight to Phoenix," Jerry answered, "and Carl's gone to Denver. In the morning Carl's got a flight to Reno and I'm flying a couple over to Vegas."

The telephone rang then, and another day of work was underway for Lisa. She finished at five in the afternoon, but rather than stay (as she often did in order to get in some flying time), she went directly to her cottage on the beach. It had been a hectic day, and after the confusion of the weekend she didn't feel in the mood for even her favorite pastime.

Lisa was in the kitchen broiling a piece of white fish and tossing a salad for her dinner when the doorbell rang. She turned off the oven and hurried down the hall to answer it.

"Good evening—my name is Gil Ramsey and I'm from the *Los Angeles Herald Examiner.*" A lanky man with close-cropped sandy hair took a card out of his shirt pocket and passed it under her nose. "Miss Lisa Palmer?"

"Yes."

"May I come in, Miss Palmer?"

That was the beginning.

Reporter after reporter, calling her on the phone, coming to her cottage, arriving at Southern Pacific Airways. How many interviews could she give?

She decided not to give any. That was her first mistake.

"I think you should get in touch with Brian Sommervale," Mark advised. "He'll know how to handle all this."

She thought seriously about it, but in the end she decided not to bother him. That was her second mistake.

❋   ❋   ❋

Lisa pulled into the police station parking lot just as two patrol cars with a group of reporters inside drove away. She jumped out of her car and ran inside the building. A tall, broad-shouldered man with shining black hair was standing at the sergeant's desk. He wore tailored white slacks, a yellow sport shirt, and wire-rimmed glasses with lightly tinted lenses. When he saw Lisa he came across the floor to meet her.

"Brian, are you all right?" she asked.

"Yes, I'm fine."

"What happened when they brought you in here?" She looked past him to the police sergeant. He was seated behind a neat desk, holding his head in his hands and rocking back and forth in his chair.

"The sergeant's a little upset," Brian said. "Why don't we get out of here and leave him alone?" He took her by the arm, and before she knew it he hurried her out the door and over to her car. He opened the door for her, then went around and climbed in the passenger's seat. She left the parking lot and pulled onto the street before he spoke. "Why didn't you call me like I told you? You still have the number I gave you, don't you?"

"Yes. And I've been thinking about calling you."

"You should have called me when all this started. I've been away on a short trip. I only heard about your trouble late last night. You've been having quite a time, haven't you?"

"It's been pretty hectic. Vic lost his temper when he came in today and found a room full of reporters. I'm afraid I wasn't getting much work done. Then when you arrived just as the police were arresting everyone, Vic didn't recognize you in all the confusion. And before I could—''

Brian chuckled, ''There's a lot of that going around. I must be taking too many trips.''

Lisa glanced over at him. She knew he was referring to the police officers who hadn't recognized him either. But he seemed to be taking it all well enough. And the policemen had had to get rough with some of the reporters. They had thought Brian was one of them. She didn't like to remember the way they had shoved him into the back of one of their cars and driven off before she could stop them.

''What happened at the police station?''

Brian summarized what had occurred, ending with, ''I really wish you'd called me.''

She wished she had too now. ''The police commissioner is a personal friend of yours? No wonder that police sergeant looked so sick when we left!''

''He was only doing his job. But I want to know why you didn't call me.''

Something in the tone of his voice prompted her to take her eyes from the road again to look at him. She could see the displeasure in his dark eyes even through the tinted lenses of his glasses. Brian Sommervale was unhappy with her, and she couldn't bear the thought of that.

''I'm sorry. I just didn't want to bother you.''

''Let's get something straight right now,'' he began, and her usual sunny glow seemed to fade at his sudden show of forcefulness. ''You are not a bother to me. I owe you my life, and the least I can do is help you out when you're in trouble, especially when the trouble has something to do with me. Now, I want you to promise me again that if you ever need me for anything you'll let me know.''

''All right. I promise,'' she said quietly.

Brian stared at her a moment, then suddenly peals of laughter shook his broad shoulders. Lisa glanced at him, marveling at that all-consuming laugh of his. If joyful was

an appropriate word to describe a Christian, then Brian
Sommervale was the happiest Christian she had ever
known—even when he was angry.

"What's so funny?" she asked softly.

"You," he said. "You should see the expression on your
face. You look like a frightened bird that just fell out of its
nest."

"Well, you're angry with me."

"I'm not angry," he said, sobering. "I have a quick temper
and you'll know it if I lose it, which isn't often. But I do want
you to know that I mean what I say."

"But I just can't bother you. You're so busy."

He shook his dark head. "You're really something, you
know that?"

"What do you mean?"

"Nothing," he laughed again. "Just forget it. But we're going
to hold a press conference," he told her then. "If we had in
the first place, you wouldn't be having all this trouble now."

At Southern Pacific Airways, Lisa parked next to Brian's
silver Imperial.

"I'll see you day after tomorrow," he said when they
climbed out. "I'll pick you up early. Don't worry about
breakfast. We'll eat at my place."

"What?"

"The press conference. It's all arranged. We're having it
at ten o'clock Saturday morning. That's day after tomorrow."

"Must we have it so soon?"

Brian gazed deeply into the appeal in her eyes. Wearing
high-heeled shoes, she stood almost at his eye level, making
it easy for him to study the vivid green of her eyes, swirling
before him like a beautiful, timeless sea. "You want to get
it over with, don't you?" he finally said.

"Well, yes. But next week would be soon enough."

Brian ran his tongue along the edges of his teeth. Then his
full lips broadened into a smile. "I'll see you Saturday. Say,

why don't you plan to stay the weekend? My sister is here. And Elena will be over."

"Elena Morrow? I've read about the two of you."

"You can't believe all that stuff. We're just good friends." He paused a moment. "You'll stay then?"

"Oh, I—"

"My mother and father will still be here too, and I know they'd like an opportunity to get to know you better. So it's all settled."

"Well, all right."

❋   ❋   ❋

Lisa was barely home from work when Sue and Mark stopped by. They had more or less adopted Lisa since she had come to California, looking out for her almost as they would a sister, and she had fallen into the habit of sharing everything with them. So this night she invited them to stay and eat with her, and over the dinner table she shared the day's events, pausing occasionally to absorb outrageous comments from Sue.

"Your life's sure been a riot since you met Brian Sommervale," she observed.

"Not to mention *his* life," Lisa added in her soft drawl. "I guess it isn't every day that he gets taken to jail." They laughed and Lisa continued, "Oh, I almost forgot to tell you— Brian invited me to spend the weekend at his estate. And guess who else will be there?"

"Who?" asked Sue with a wide-eyed expression.

"Elena Morrow."

"The movie star! Wow, Lisa, you'll be rubbing elbows with the upper crust. She's one of the fastest rising starlets in Hollywood!"

"I don't know if I should go," Lisa debated. "I have to go to the press conference, I suppose, but maybe I shouldn't stay afterward."

"Go ahead, you'll have a wonderful time," Sue said. "And be sure to call me next week and tell me all about it."

"Brian really didn't give me much of a chance to say no. He seems so nice. I think he really must be a wonderful person."

"Do you really think he's wonderful?" Sue asked.

"I really hardly know him, but he seems to be everything his reputation says. But...well...what difference does it make?"

"He's single, and that means he's fair game."

Lisa laughed. "You make him sound like one of those sitting ducks at a shooting gallery."

"He is, my friend. All men are—haven't you learned that yet?"

"She's right," Mark put in. "We're just poor, helpless creatures waiting to be plucked from the vine of life by some dewy-eyed female."

"Oh, sure!" said Lisa. "You're about as helpless as an angry barracuda."

"Your compliments are astounding."

"But Brian Sommervale," Sue said. "You're crazy to pass up a chance like that!"

"I couldn't even think of such a thing. Brian Sommervale is so...well, he's so special. I could never think of him that way."

"Then maybe he'll think of it."

"You have such an imagination, Sue. A man like Brian Sommervale would never be interested in someone like me. He's just being nice to me because I saved his life."

Chapter 4 ✿✿✿✿✿✿✿✿✿✿✿✿

*B*rian parked his car in the paved drive bordered on each side with bright, golden poppies. In the yard stood sturdy yuccas, with their woody trunks, pointed leaves, and clusters of bell-shaped flowers. Here and there a lofty palm waved its rich green fronds in the slight breeze. Sun splashed this idyllic scene, and in the distance white-capped waves peaked and broke over the sandy shore. Brian climbed out and mounted the few steps of the low porch to the yellow concrete block house. Around the porch were the same colorful poppies that decorated the length of the driveway. He pressed the bell button and Lisa welcomed him at once with a wide, eager smile.

"Good morning!"

"Good morning! You look great!"

"Thank you."

For her encounter with the press, Lisa had chosen to wear a sleeveless navy dress with a high white midriff. She had pulled her shoulder-length blonde hair to the back of her head in a becoming arrangement of curls, and had pinned a red rose at the side of her hair. She had on navy high-heeled sandals.

Brian stepped into the living room and Lisa closed the door behind him. He wore tailored white slacks and a blue silk shirt that enhanced the dark, rich color of his hair and offset the deep, even tan of his skin.

"I'm all ready to go—I think," she said.

He regarded her with a speculative gaze for a moment. Then he left her side and tramped around her little house like a restless lion.

"This place really is small," he observed, coming back to her.

"It's just right for me. You're just used to that palace you live in."

"Maybe so, but I'd get claustrophobia in here."

"You're exaggerating."

"Your place is real nice," he said. "I'm only kidding."

She gazed fondly at him.

"Wouldn't you like a bigger place?"

Her mouth fell open with surprise. What could he be thinking of?

She shook her blonde curls. "No, Brian. Absolutely not—"

"Calm down— I get the message."

"You wouldn't? I mean—"

"Of course not. If you don't want me to."

"Oh, I don't. I couldn't."

Imagine, thought Lisa, this man could go out and buy houses the way most people buy clothes or toys for their children! She sighed audibly. Was all this really happening to her?

"We'd better be going," Brian said, and walked over to her single piece of luggage sitting by the door. "Is this all you're taking? Most women would have a trunk."

"Just for the weekend?"

"That's what I mean." He picked up the bag and opened the door. She stood back.

"Aren't you coming?"

"Do I have to?"

"Yes, you have to," he said, smiling and imitating the sound of her soft feminine drawl. "Why are you so reluctant about the press conference?"

"I don't know. I've never been involved in such a thing before."

"There's nothing to it. Now come on."

"It's not too late to call it off, is it?"

The commanding Brian would have none of Lisa's procrastinations. "March!" he said, motioning toward the door with her suitcase.

"No!" she flared with a teasing little smile.

Brian looked surprised. But only for a moment. "Young lady, are you talking back to me? Haven't you learned that nobody talks back to Brian Sommervale?"

She stared at him, then began to laugh. "You look funny when you're trying to act bossy."

"Bossy? Is that what you think I am? Why, I ought to turn you over my knee."

"You wouldn't dare!"

He set the luggage on the floor. But when he started in her direction, she said, "Okay, okay. I won't talk back any more."

"I get enough sass from my sister. I don't need any more from you."

She grinned at him again. "I thought you said *nobody* talks back to you."

He laughed. "She hasn't learned that yet either. Now come on, little girl, let's go."

"Who are you calling a 'little girl'? I'm—"

"You're acting like a little girl."

Lisa gathered herself up and strode primly out the door, pretending to sulk. Stifling a shout of amused laughter, Brian picked up her suitcase and followed. Once outside her mood changed.

"That's not the same car you were driving day before yesterday," she said, regarding the green-colored spectacle in her driveway.

"It's a 1931 Cord L29 Sedan. There aren't many of them in existence."

"I can see why."

Brian chuckled as he put her bag in the trunk. Then he went around to open the door for her to get into the front seat. On the driver's side he climbed in beside her.

"Do you have a lot of cars?" she asked, settling herself in the elaborate green-and-white leather interior.

"Just this one and the Imperial I drove the other day and a Lotus Europa."

"A what?"

He backed out of the drive and started up the road. "It's a sports car."

"Whose sports car passed me the other day when I was leaving your house?"

"That must have been my sister, Heather."

"She sure must have been in a hurry. She was driving like the devil himself was after her."

"Sometimes I think he's gaining on her. Does the name Eric Williams mean anything to you?"

"No, I don't think so."

"He was a popular race car driver."

"Oh, yes, now I remember. He was killed about a year ago in a race. I read about it in the paper. It was a terrible accident."

"Heather was his wife."

"Oh, I'm so sorry."

"When Eric died I think my sister went kind of crazy. She's still a spoiled child in a lot of ways."

"Doesn't she have a young son?"

"Eric Jr. He's the image of his father. Sometimes I wonder if this helps Heather or hurts her. I've never seen a woman love a man the way she loved Eric."

"How did you escape being a spoiled child?"

He flicked a glance at her, a jolly expression behind his tinted lenses. "Who says I escaped? Sure I'm spoiled. Completely rotten."

"You can't be very spoiled and do the things you do."

"What's that got to do with it? I enjoy everything I have."

"Brian, may I ask you a personal question?"

"Sure. Ask me anything you like."

"Why do you go around giving away your money?"

He was a long moment in answering, and his mood changed totally when he did. "Jesus said that when you do something for the least of these, you do it for me. He said that if you *don't* do it for these, you don't do it for me. I give it away because it's needed. I try to help the desperately needy who can't help themselves, and I try to help those who can and are making some effort. It's really not all that complicated or mysterious. Basically I'm just a guy with a lot of money who doesn't like to see people suffer."

"If I may ask, how was the Sommervale fortune acquired?"

"It was acquired by my great-grandfather. He invented some kind of device used in mining. From there it was a matter of wise investments—real estate, corporations, all the usual things. Dad runs the business now from his office in San Francisco." He took his eyes from the road to glance briefly at her. "He gets a kick out of telling people how he makes the money and how his son tries to give it all away."

They laughed and Lisa said, "You're a rare person, Brian."

He reached out and placed his hand over hers. "I'm glad you think so." She smiled and he said, "Whatever I am, if I'm anything at all, I owe to God and my parents. Like you, my parents gave me God. They started me out under His direction, and I'm grateful that I was brought up to believe and to have respect for all people. That's another debt I can never repay."

"Another debt?"

"Like the one I owe you for saving my life?"

"You don't owe me anything. I told you that."

"I know what you told me, but that doesn't change the way I feel."

"You must be overwhelmed with needs and demands in your work," she said, trying to bring up a new topic. "How do you handle them all?"

"No matter how many needs are brought to my attention, I can only handle them one at a time, because the personal involvement is so important to me. I pray over each situation. Some needs are more urgent than others, and I rely on God to guide me."

"Brian, this will probably sound stupid, but how does it feel to be so wealthy? I can't imagine it."

"I don't know how it *feels.* I was born wealthy. I don't have anything to compare it with except what I see around me. As I said, I enjoy everything I have. But is it all really mine, or on loan to me from God while I'm here? I've got more money than I'll ever need, and if you'll excuse an old cliché, I'm not going to take any of it with me when I leave. So maybe I can spread a little of it around while I'm here."

Brian Sommervale's 150-acre estate was a vast affair of breathtaking greenery facing palm-lined Brenthall Drive. The rear of his estate extended along an open stretch of beach where the rolling tide bathed the shore in a murmur of foam and softness.

Brian brought his car to a stop before the entrance of the majestic grounds. He reached toward the dashboard and pushed a button. Instantly the wrought-iron gates swung open and he drove through. The gates closed behind them, and as they rode up the graceful, winding drive to the house Lisa glanced around, her emerald eyes wide with wonder at the beauty surrounding them. Towering oak trees, hanging heavy with verdurous leaves, lined each side of the blacktop road, and acres of landscaped lushness stretched out in every direction as far as she could see.

Brian parked his sedan along the curve in the drive which lay parallel to the great veranda of the mansion, with its giant square posts running from the floor to the balcony alcove.

The mansion, a giant version of a typical Southern California home, consisted of whitewashed stucco with orange tile roofing. Separate wings extended from each side of the main portion of the two-story house, and an abundance of black wrought iron decorated the arched doorways and windows.

At the broad double doors of the house Lisa and Brian were met by an enormous, long-limbed man. "Morning, folks," he greeted with a big white grin.

"You remember Lisa," Brian said as they stepped into the foyer.

The butler nodded agreeably. "Yes, sir! None of us will ever forget Lisa!"

"Peter, you'll find Lisa's bag in the back of the car," Brian said. "And you'd better move my car for the reporters."

"Yes, sir," the butler answered, and in two great strides his towering frame went past them and out the door.

Brian led Lisa past a splendid curving staircase and down the hall to a paneled recreation-and-game room. Through an archway a patio overlooked a gigantic pool which formed a large circle at one end, then narrowed and opened to a smaller circle at the other end. They walked outside and stood gazing at the shimmering blue water. It lay quiet and beautiful before them in the early sunlight that streamed through the surrounding palms. In the distance white surf lapped gently at the edge of the sandy beach.

"Your home is magnificent, Brian," Lisa said, "and this pool is too lovely and inviting."

"Thank you. Do you swim?"

Realizing his comic intent, she said, "Not very well, actually. Perhaps you could give me a few pointers some time."

Bursting into laughter, Brian said, "I *can* swim, you know."

"I'm sure you can."

"I just get a little hysterical when beautiful blondes start slapping me around."

They laughed again and walked the length of the patio to a table near the small end of the pool. Seated around the glass-top table were Brian's parents and his secretary. Helen Sommervale was a petite woman with skillfully coiffed silver-gray hair and sparkling hazel eyes. Brian's father was as tall and muscular as his son and had the same shining black hair, now sprinkled with gray, and the same dark, graphic eyes, alert behind rimless glasses.

During breakfast Lisa again felt the warmth that had drawn her to the Sommervales on her first visit to Brian's home. And his secretary, an attractive middle-aged woman with dark hair and bright blue eyes, made her feel even more welcome.

When Livy, the Sommervale's cook, came out from the kitchen to greet Lisa, she was reminded of the scene she had witnessed in the rear courtyard when she had driven Brian home after the storm. The millionaire had greeted his plump cook as if she were his mother, throwing his arms around her and kissing her shiny cheeks. What a wonderful household this was, thought Lisa. And how fortunate she was to be a guest here!

In the powder room off the main foyer, Lisa took a few minutes to freshen her face before Peter announced the arrival of the media people. Then Brian and she entered the living room together, her eyes taking in every lavish segment. A massive stone fireplace occupied one entire wall, and opposite the hearth sat a long, white velvet couch decorated with red-and-blue scatter pillows. A white grand piano stood in one corner by an arched doorway that opened onto a side veranda. Two red velvet loveseats faced each other in another corner, and heavy dark-blue drapes hung at the tall, curved windows. Expensive paintings adorned the creamy white walls, and a plush dark-blue carpet graced the floor.

Brian and Lisa seated themselves on the couch. In front of them stood four men and three women, armed with pad and pen and an unshakable curiosity that was prominent on their faces.

The press conference went well, with Brian publicly thanking everyone for the interest in his welfare, and Lisa being asked to describe the events that led to the present day. Then the reporters asked a few personal questions.

"Is there someone special in your life, Miss Palmer?" one of the women asked.

"Not right now."

"Not even a young man back home?" a man pressed her.

"There's no one special."

"What about you, Mr. Sommervale?" asked a young man. "Are you planning to marry Elena Morrow?"

"Not today," Brian retorted, and drew a number of smiles from the men and women of the press.

"What do you have against marriage, Mr. Sommervale?" a lady asked. "You've seemed reluctant to give up your bachelor state."

"I don't have anything against marriage," said Brian. "I think it's a great institution. I'm just not ready to do time in it yet."

This reply brought laughter from everyone, and then on a serious note Brian said, "To give you a completely honest answer, it would take a very special woman to share my kind of life and work. And frankly, I haven't been looking. But if I ever find her and fall in love, you can bet I'll marry her—if she'll have me."

After a few more questions, Brian politely brought the interview to an end. He rose with Lisa beside him as the reporters thanked them for their time and prepared to leave.

"May we get some pictures, Mr. Sommervale?" a woman asked.

The throng trouped out to the front veranda, where Lisa posed beside Brian. They were about to finish when one of the women spoke up.

"Come on, Mr. Sommervale, be the good sport we know you are and show the world how much you appreciate what the beautiful young lady did for you."

Brian glanced at Lisa and winked. "Come here, little girl," he said, reaching over and closing an arm about her waist. Then he proceeded to plant a kiss, strong and true, on her startled lips.

Flashbulbs popped everywhere and then the media people got in their cars and left, laughing and absolutely satisfied with the interview.

Lisa turned on Brian in a huff. "Just why did you do that?" she flared.

"I never have shown you how really grateful I am for all you did," he said into her stormy green eyes.

"I thought you were a gentleman. I didn't know you carried on like this."

He pretended a shameful face. Then his features broke into a playful grin and she started to laugh. She couldn't stay angry with this man whose crooked little smile made her heart turn somersaults.

In the foyer Brian took Lisa by the hand. "Come with me, Lisa. I want to show you something."

He led her down a thick, carpeted hallway and into a darkly paneled office. A massive desk sat before a broad window that framed a majestic view of the beautiful Pacific, and across from the desk two dark brown leather chairs flanked a wall of bookshelves.

"Look at these," Brian said, walking over to his desk. He picked up a stack of letters and telegrams. "These are all because of you," he said, pointing to more stacks nearby. "People expressing their gratitude for my safety."

"All those letters and telegrams are because of you, not me. Everyone loves you, and rightly so."

He put down the letters and took her hands in his. "You're very sweet, and I thank you for caring." He bent slightly and placed a kiss of infinite tenderness on her mouth. "That's not for the world—that's just from me to you." They gazed at each other for a long, engrossing moment, until finally Brian's clear baritone broke the stillness. "Why don't you go change and we'll go for a swim."

Lisa smiled her agreement, and they left the office and started along the hall.

"I'll have Maude show you to your room. I'll meet you on the patio."

In the foyer Brian left his guest and disappeared through a door to the left. Seconds later his secretary joined Lisa in the entrance hall.

"Come with me," Maude said smiling. "Peter put your bag in one of the guest rooms upstairs."

Lisa followed Maude's trim figure up the winding staircase to the plush corridor of the west wing, where she showed her into a spacious room done in a French Provincial decor. A white canopy bed covered in pink satin was the focal point of the bedroom, and on the adjacent wall sat a matching dresser. A deep closet occupied the wall next to a private bath that contained a pink sunken tub. Across the room French doors led to a long balcony which held a glorious view of the crescent-shaped beach. A complementary lounge in deep shades of pink completed the room.

As soon as Maude had gone, Lisa went over to the balcony doors, throwing them open to take in the beauty of the view below. Then she turned back to admire the lovely room again. It was hard to believe that she was actually in Brian Sommervale's home and that she had been invited for the entire weekend. What other wonders could life possibly hold for her?

Lisa changed into a two-piece, floral print swimsuit and put on the matching coat, then hurried down to the patio. Brian was nowhere in sight when she arrived, so she sat down in a comfortable chair by the pool to wait. Soon she heard

footsteps behind her and turned to see a boy about five years
of age staring at her from a few feet away. His blonde hair
curled all over the top of his head and his brown eyes were
so dark they seemed almost black. A childlike expression of
innocence and inquiry monopolized his round face.

"Hi! My name's Eric."

"Hello, Eric. I'm Lisa." She smiled kindly at him and he
moved closer.

"You're the lady who saved Uncle Brian's life. Do you
know my mommy?"

"No, I don't, Eric, but I'm looking forward to meeting her."

"She's not here right now." He examined her outfit from
his great dark eyes. "Are you going swimming?"

"Your uncle and I are going swimming."

"Can I go too? I'll have to ask Uncle Brian."

"Ask Uncle Brian what?" the philanthropist said, coming
across the patio in trim white trunks that heightened the
bronze color of his graceful, solid body.

"Can I go swimming?" Eric asked, running up to him.

Brian bent down and scooped the boy into his strong arms.
"I think that would be fine. What do you think, Lisa?"

"I think so too."

"Oh, boy!" Eric cried, hopping down and racing for the
door. "I'll be right back!"

"He seems like an adorable child," Lisa said as soon as the
boy had disappeared inside the house.

"He's a real joy in my life," Brian said. "He's been with
us most of the time since my brother-in-law was killed.
Heather can't seem to bring herself to go back to her home
in Lake Tahoe for any length of time, so she's been alternating
stays between here and our parents' home in San Francisco.
When she decides to leave permanently, I'm going to miss
Eric very much. Even though I'm gone a lot, I look forward
to coming home and finding him here."

"You'd make a wonderful father, Brian. You should get

married and fill this big house with children."

"When I find that special woman—*if* I find her," he said
into her eyes. The expression Lisa saw there seemed to hold
her attention, occupying it wholly. The spell was broken only
when Eric came charging onto the patio wearing scarlet swimming trunks and a wide, happy grin.

"I'm all ready, Uncle Brian!"

Brian watched the child in silence as he ran to the edge
of the pool. "And when we decide to start our family," he
said to Lisa, "I'll limit my travels. Not the needs, but the
traveling. The last thing I want my children to have is an
absentee father."

"Come on, Uncle Brian!" Eric called, "I'll race ya!"

"I haven't been in since that little dunking I took last
weekend," he informed his guest, "but I can't let a little thing
like the Pacific Ocean get me down."

Brian took off his glasses and laid them on a nearby table.
Then Eric and he dived into the heated pool and swam its
swirling length. Lisa looked on for a moment before removing
her beach coat and plunging her tall, lithe form in after them.

It was Peter's announcement that lunch would soon be
served that brought them from the water some time later.
Lisa was first to climb out, with Eric emerging behind her.

"You're a regular little fish," she told him.

"He takes to water like a duck," Brian said, coming up the
ladder after them.

"It's too bad you don't," Lisa teased as she picked up one
of the towels and started to dry herself.

Lisa's golden hair and tawny skin glistened brightly in the
afternoon sun, and Brian took a minute to admire her fresh,
sparkling beauty. "Oh, is that so," he replied, moving to her
side. Then he grabbed her towel and began rubbing her
briskly about the head.

"Would you just look at this!" came a woman's voice from
the other side of the patio.

Chapter 5 ✳✳✳✳✳✳✳✳✳✳✳✳

*B*rian glanced up, bringing his playful rubdown to a halt. He ran one hand through his shining black hair, still damp and gleaming from the swim, and his full lips parted into a smile.

"You fool with me, young lady, and I'll give you some of the same." He strode with a carefree bounce over to the woman and gave her an affectionate kiss on the cheek.

Elena Morrow was even more beautiful in person than in the movies, thought Lisa. She had her long auburn hair tied up in a scarf, and her violet blue eyes were as lustrous as her flawless complexion. The smile on her face revealed her beautiful white teeth, and her bright orange pantsuit enhanced her famous figure.

Eric strolled up to the movie star and she bent to kiss him on his wet head. "Hello, sweetheart."

"We've been swimming!"

"Yes, I see you have," she said, giving Brian an exasperated look which he completely ignored.

A slim woman came through the door to get Eric ready for lunch. Elena Morrow spoke to the maid and then looked past her to Brian. "I thought after last weekend you'd never go near the water again, but here you are—"

"If there's one thing I can't stand," Brian broke in good-naturedly, "it's a woman who nags." He turned back to Lisa.

"You'll have to pardon Elena—she's terrified of water, which gets to be a lot of fun when she has a swim scene in one of her films."

The movie star gave Brian a look of patient tolerance and addressed Lisa: "And you'll have to pardon Brian's manners for not introducing us." She crossed the patio with long, graceful strides. "I'm Elena Morrow. And you must be Lisa."

The two women shook hands. "How do you do?" Lisa said. "I'm very pleased to meet you." She gazed curiously at the beautiful movie queen for a moment, wondering what the woman thought of the playful scene she had just interrupted. She didn't seem concerned, and Brian had said Elena and he were only friends. Still, Lisa felt uncomfortable, as if she had been caught in some guilty act.

"Come, Lisa, let's sit down," Elena Morrow said. "We must get acquainted."

"If you'll excuse me, I'll go in and change," Brian said, picking up his glasses from the table nearby and starting for the door.

Lisa and Elena sat down on a cushioned loveseat not far from the doorway. "I want to commend you for what you did for Brian," the star began.

"Oh, Miss Morrow, I—"

"Call me Elena, please. And I hope it's all right that I call you Lisa."

This woman certainly wasn't anything like Lisa's concept of a Hollywood star. She was another of those amiable, unassuming types with which Brian seemed to surround himself.

"Yes, of course. And I hope you don't think—Elena—that Brian and I...well, when you arrived—"

"Oh, for heaven's sake. Brian and I are just friends—the best of friends, but only friends."

"I didn't know what you might think."

"I don't think anything. But I'd love to see Brian fall in

love and get married. And who better than the woman who saved his life?"

"Oh, my goodness!" cried Lisa. "I don't...I mean Brian and I...it could never be like that."

"Don't be awed by Brian's position, Lisa," Elena said. "For all his unique qualities, he's still a man like any other. Well, not exactly like any other. He's the most special person I know." She smiled, showing her beautiful teeth. "As I was saying, you're to be commended for what you did. Most people wouldn't have had that much fortitude."

"I'm sure they would have, but thank you anyway. Were you on the yacht with Brian?"

"No, thank God. I don't indulge very often. After what happened to him, I may never go out again. Now tell me, how did the press conference go?"

Lisa told Elena some of what had taken place, ending with the pictures on the front veranda.

"I can't wait to see the morning papers," Elena said, looking up as Brandon Sommervale came onto the patio with his arm around his wife. "Lisa and I have been getting to know each other," Elena told them. "She's just been telling me about the press conference."

"Brian was pleased with the way it went," Helen Sommervale said.

Especially those pictures, thought Lisa with a smile. She rose. "If you'll excuse me, I'd better go in and get ready for lunch."

That afternoon Brian took Lisa around to the stable area, where he kept his Arabian horses. A gleaming white stallion delighted in parading around the corral as they looked on, and a beautiful chestnut mare nuzzled Lisa's arm as she stroked her well-shaped head. In the nearby pasture two gray geldings grazed.

Being a long-time equestrienne raised in the Lone Star State, Lisa immediately fell in love with the splendid group of horses and couldn't wait to go for a ride. Brian had the chestnut mare saddled for her and the white stallion saddled for himself, and they galloped up and down the beach to the tune of the rolling tide and cantered over the seemingly endless acres of shaded greenery that made up the larger portion of Brian's estate.

When they returned from their ride late in the afternoon, Elena and an athletic Mr. Sommervale were playing a game of tennis on the south lawn below the pool. Lisa and Brian stopped to watch, but the game was called to an abrupt halt when Elena was summoned to the telephone. Everyone walked up to the house, where Maude and Mrs. Sommervale joined them from the pool; they sat on the patio refreshing themselves with tall, cool glasses of iced tea and lemonade.

"That was my agent calling," Elena said as she rejoined the group. She took a seat next to Brian. "I have the most wonderful news." She glanced at the millionaire. "You know I told you the studio's been trying to get Jeffrey Stewart to direct my next film." Brian nodded and she went on. "He'll be flying over from London in June."

"That's great!" Brian said.

"He's a brilliant director," Elena told the gathering. "He's young—early thirties, I think. I haven't worked with him before, but they say he's absolutely marvelous."

That evening after a spectacular feast, which Livy proudly announced was especially in honor of Lisa, everyone adjourned to the living room for coffee. Later, while Brian played, they gathered around the grand piano standing in the corner and sang favorite songs.

Early Sunday morning Brian woke up the entire household and ushered them into the living room to look at the picture of Lisa and himself on the front page of the newspaper.

"I just played it up a little for the reporters," he explained.

Lisa stared at the picture of Brian kissing her. What would

people think of them? Her cheeks flamed when she considered that people might think they were becoming romantically involved.

After church service at a chapel in Brenthall where Brian was a member, Peter served dinner in the spacious dining room furnished with a heavy oak table and matching buffet. Tapestry drapes of green and gold were drawn to each side of full, arched windows, and a crystal chandelier that hung from the ceiling caught the reflection of the gold velvet chair seats, making distorted shapes dance on the printed paper covering the walls.

The meal was about to come to an end when the double doors of the dining room flew open and Heather burst upon the gathering. She gripped a wrinkled newspaper in a not-too-steady hand.

"Well, what do we have here?" she asked, sauntering over to the table. "A little cozy family dinner, I presume. And this must be the newest member of the family." She made her way over to Lisa, seated beside Brian.

It was obvious that Brian's sister had had too much to drink, and he couldn't be sure what she might say in her intoxicated condition, so he prepared himself for anything. When he had told Heather about Lisa saving his life, she had reacted with her typical skepticism, accusing Lisa of being interested only in a montary reward for what she had done, and suggesting that his gratitude was making him seem like a lovesick schoolboy.

Was that what was happening to him? Was he falling in love with the wonderful young woman who had rescued him? He turned to smile at her, and deep in his heart began a fresh, new song.

"Aren't you going to introduce me?" Heather demanded of her brother. Inclining her dark head defiantly, she gazed down on Lisa with eyes that burned like a seething volcano. "Never mind," she told Brian. "I'll introduce myself. I'm

Heather Williams, sister to The Super Altruist. And don't tell me, you're—how did you describe her, Brian? Oh, yes—the lovely, willowy Lisa. You take a good picture." As a final affront to Lisa's presence, Heather flung the newspaper on the table in front of her. Lisa sat dumbfounded, staring up at the woman with liquored breath who was leaning over her.

"I know your type," Heather went on, "with your Sunday school manners and your—"

Brian was out of his chair. "That's enough!" he said, taking his sister not too gently by the arm. "Come on."

Heather shook her head violently. "Leave me alone! I'm only doing what any good sister would do. She's helping herself to your food, and soon she'll be dipping into your pocket."

"I said that's enough!" Brian stormed, and Lisa saw some of his quick temper flashing in his dark eyes. He tightened his grip on Heather's arm and pulled her toward the door. She tried to free herself from his grasp, but he held her firmly, saying, "Come on, let's go upstairs and sleep it off."

Heather's performance had sent Lisa's good spirits into a plunge, but when Brian returned to the table, apologizing for his sister, Eric asked him to take them up in his Lear jet. Brian asked Lisa and Elena to join them, and after they were airborne he called Lisa into the cockpit and let her take over the controls.

Livy had supper waiting when the little group returned from their short flight, and after the meal everyone adjourned to the veranda off the living room. Heather came downstairs later and found them involved in idle talk. Conversation ceased abruptly as she came outside and stopped before Lisa's chair.

Lisa looked up uncertainly into a face that was tired and drawn. In spite of the beauty still in her features, Heather had amassed a sallow, withered look, and a close examination of her dark eyes revealed a pain harbored deep in her soul.

"Please accept my apology, Lisa," she said, "I'm afraid I made a scene this afternoon."

"You don't have to apologize, Mrs. Williams," Lisa said.

"I know I don't have to," Heather snapped, "but in view of what you did for my brother, I'd better or I'll be in the doghouse around here." She turned to Brian seated nearby. "Where's Peter? Eric's looking for him to go riding."

"I don't know, Heather."

"I don't know what good it does you to have servants—they're never around when you need them. Which isn't surprising, the way you treat them. Servants aren't supposed to be treated like members of the family."

"As a guest in your brother's home, Heather dear," Helen Sommervale said, "you shouldn't criticize his household."

"I'm not a guest, I'm his sister!" her daughter retorted, glancing at Lisa. "The Olympic swimmer here is a guest."

Brian ran his tongue along the edges of his teeth. Then he smiled. "Yes, and I'm glad you're showing her your good side."

Heather frowned at him and took a seat next to Elena.

"Heather, your mother and I will be going home tomorrow or the next day," Mr. Sommervale said. "Why don't you and Eric come and stay with us for awhile?"

"What's the matter? Brian getting tired of me?"

"How could I get tired of you?" Brian said. "You aren't here that much, but I wish you'd spend more time with Eric."

"What would you know about spending time with somebody?" Heather spat. "The altruistic Mr. Sommervale, our Benevolent Benefactor. Ah, correction, our Self-appointed Benevolent Benefactor, who's always running off somewhere doing something for some poor slob he doesn't even know."

"It's a thankless job, but somebody's got to do it," Brian returned with a look of patient good humor in his eyes.

"Heather dear—" Helen Sommervale began.

"Oh, don't lecture me, Mother." She flicked her glance to

Elena, and Lisa wondered what had happened to Brian's wonderful household. It seemed that Heather had a way of disrupting the peaceful atmosphere.

"When do you start your new film?" Heather asked the movie star.

"In June. Lance Whitworth and I are working together again. And we have a brilliant director coming over from London."

"Oh? Who's that?"

"Jeffrey Stewart."

Heather brightened suddenly. *"The* Jeffrey Stewart?"

"Yes, do you know him?"

"Eric and I met him in New York one time," she said, a clever gleam coming into her dark eyes. She glanced at Lisa. "If you think my brother is something, wait till you get a look at Jeffrey Stewart. He looks like some great Greek god. He's as tall as a statue and his eyes are as blue as the sky. And his voice. I've never heard anything like it. It sort of caresses you, like the touch of velvet next to your skin." She turned back to the movie star. "You'll love working with him, Elena. He has the sweetest temperament. He never gets overbearing the way Brian sometimes does."

The philanthropist gave his sister a disarming smile, and Elena said, "Sounds like you remember Jeffrey Stewart pretty well, Heather."

"A man like that a woman could never forget," she said dreamily.

"Heather dear, I do wish you'd come home with us for awhile," Mrs. Sommervale persisted again.

"I will, Mother, later." She smiled slowly, delightfully. "I think I'll stick around here awhile longer. Life is starting to get interesting again."

Chapter 6 ❀❀❀❀❀❀❀❀❀❀❀❀❀

*T*he week that followed the visit to Brian's estate was a diligent but calmer one for Lisa. She received notes and telephone calls from kind people wanting to thank her for what she had done in rescuing Brian. And even the teasing she had to endure from Vic and Jerry about the picture in the Sunday paper seemed mild compared to the aggravation of the media people.

At the end of the week Lisa was cleaning house, humming a favorite hymn as she worked. The ringing of the doorbell brought her dustcloth to an abrupt halt on the coffee table. She went to the front window and peeked out between the floral drapes. A man in a brown uniform stood at the door and a large van with another uniformed man sitting at the wheel was parked in the driveway. The name "Elison's Department Store" was printed on the side of the van in huge brown letters.

Later Lisa was standing in the middle of the living room floor, still in a state of shock, when the telephone rang. She went slowly down the hall to the bedroom to answer it.

"Oh, Brian, what have you done?"

He laughed his beautiful deep laugh. "Do you like it?"

"It's wonderful. But I can't accept such an extravagant gift."

"Why not?"

"Well, because...because it's so expensive."

"You'll have to come up with something better than that," he chuckled.

"Well, I can't, that's all. It's wonderful of you, but—"

"Hush," he broke in. "I bought it for your little house. I noticed you didn't have anything like that. No TV or anything."

"But a home entertainment center! Brian, it's—"

"I said hush. It's yours. Enjoy."

"But how can I ever thank you?"

"I'm the one trying to do the thanking."

"Brian—"

"Consider it installment number one on a great debt."

"Oh, please don't—"

"Young lady, I told you I'm not accustomed to having people talk back to me, especially when I give them something."

"Yes, sir," Lisa replied limply.

"That's better. Now, what are you doing tomorrow?"

"You have to ask, after this? I can do almost anything I want."

"You can do that today. Tomorrow I'll pick you up for church and we'll come back here for dinner."

"Thank you, Brian, but you've done too much already."

"Would you rather go out to dinner? I probably like to spend too much time at home, but I'm away so much. I've been gone all this week, but if you'd rather go out—"

"Oh, no, it's not that. It's just that I can't let you do all this. I thought you understood that I didn't want you to—"

"Are you talking back to me again?"

She laughed. "No, but—"

"Good. Then I'll see you in the morning."

Lisa let out a long, deep sigh. "Brian."

"Yes."

"Thank you for the most beautiful present I've ever had."

"You're welcome, Lisa. It's a beautiful present for the most beautiful lady I know."

At the estate Lisa and Brian dined alone except for Maude. Mr. and Mrs. Sommervale had returned to their home in San Francisco, and Heather had taken Eric out for the afternoon.

Immediately following dinner, Brian excused himself and went into his office to take care of some unexpected business. He had been asked to help out with the urgent needs of some nearby flood victims. He left Lisa in the care of his secretary and they sat on the veranda off the living room sipping iced coffee from a tray Peter brought out.

Later that afternoon Brian called Maude into his office, and Lisa wandered out to the kitchen to chat with Livy. When Brian finished in his office, he asked Lisa to join him in the game room, where he taught her some of the techniques of shooting pool. They laughed and talked and had a good time playing games of pool and ping-pong.

Following a light supper, they attended evening services at church, and afterward Brian drove her home in his silver Imperial. Riding along, they discussed some points of the minister's sermon on Christians using their gifts to the fullest.

After a brief silent lapse, Lisa said, "Brian, until Maude told me some things this afternoon, I didn't really have any idea about you. Everyone's heard about the good you do— it's hard to keep it a secret, I know. But I didn't know you gave so much of *yourself* all the time. What I mean is, I didn't understand how everything touches you so deeply."

"I didn't know my loyal secretary had such a big mouth."

"What is hardest about your work? I mean what gets to you the most?"

Brian took his eyes from the road to glance briefly at her. "There's no way to accurately convey it. You'd have to see some of the sights I've seen—orphans tugging at your sleeve, begging you not to go, pleading with big, grievous eyes to go home with you; kids who eat dirt to ease the pain of star-

vation; a child sleeping in the street with the rats and roaches;
a teenage girl sexually abused by her father and too hardened
or terrified to let you come near her. It's kids who get to me,
Lisa—any child who has less than a full chance at life."

Lisa examined the profile of the man who had so dramatic-
ally entered her life, trying to find something in the contour
of his firm jaw and in the line of his straight nose that might
reveal more about the man within. What kind of man was
this, she thought, who was so sensitive to the pain of other
people? Who was this man of so much compassion, this man
with such a capacity for love that he was completely
wrapped up in other people's misery? Gazing at Brian, Lisa
realized that he embodied all that a Christian in today's world
should be. He genuinely cared about other people. As she
contemplated the man behind the prescription lenses, she
began to wonder about her own life. She had been a church
member as long as she could remember, and since coming
to California she had been leading young people in a Bible
study class. And she witnessed whenever she could—as with
Sue and Mark. But could God have something more in mind
for her? Did her unusual meeting with Brian Sommervale
have a special significance she hadn't realized?

"You've seen so much misery and sadness," Lisa finally
said. "I don't know how you bear it."

"Are you saying you wouldn't want to go with me on any
of my trips?"

This surprised her. "Were you thinking of asking me?"

"I might."

"Brian, when you see so much hurting and misery, doesn't
it make you question God? How do you explain that He can
let such atrocities go on?"

"You mean, why doesn't God do something?"

"Yes."

"He did. He sent Jesus. And His love in our hearts causes
us to want to do something. God has chosen to work through

His people to make the world a better place and to relieve the suffering and misery. We are the hands and feet, the hearts and minds He wants to use. But if we don't respond to the needs, the work doesn't get done. And people go right on suffering and being miserable.''

"You mean it's our fault so many people don't have enough to eat?''

"Americans throw away more food than many people even have. But I think we haven't accepted our responsibility in world hunger because we've never really been *hungry*. We make up 6 percent of the world's population, but we use 40 percent of the world's resources.''

"Doesn't the government help?''

"Our government has given away excess grain. Other governments sell it and use the money to build up their military. So starvation continues as a way of life and death. It's just accepted in some places. But many Christians and others are helping to meet this great need. We see a lot of good and a lot of happiness in the work I do. And believe me, the happy *always* outweighs the sad.'' He smiled his slightly crooked smile. "Listen to me. I sound like Crusader Rabbit.''

"No, you just sound like you care.''

"I get much more than I give, in terms of blessings. And the only way I can go on is in God's power. So much of what I see just rips my heart wide open, but not all of it is horrible. I have a lot of fun too. It just plain feels good to help people.

"Incidentally, next Saturday we're taking a busload of orphans to the skating rink.''

"I'll bet you're driving the bus.''

"Peter drives. That way I can get right in the middle of the kids and have a ball. Why don't you come with us?''

"I'd love to. Brian, I'm so glad I was the one who heard you calling out that night.''

He reached over and gave her hand a tender squeeze. "So am I, Lisa.''

"But you do make me ashamed."

He faced her for a moment. "I do what?"

"You do so much for others and I do so little. You're so—"

"Hey, no accolades. The work of all Christians is equally important in the sight of God. It all fits together in God's plan like the pieces of a puzzle. And only He knows what the picture will look like when the puzzle is finished."

"I know what the picture will look like," Lisa said, smiling over at him. "It'll be a picture of Jesus."

Chapter 7 ✿✿✿✿✿✿✿✿✿✿✿✿

*W*eekends at Brian Sommervale's estate soon became a way of life for Lisa. They spent many good hours in fellowship when Brian was not away on business, and their friendship grew vigorously. Lisa and Brian became constant companions, going almost everywhere together. They attended church services, civic functions, and charity dinners, and often Brian asked Lisa to accompany him on his local humanitarian endeavors to hospitals, orphanages, or nursing homes—wherever his kindness and concern was needed.

Lisa was deeply touched by Brian's kindness to her and his offer of friendship, but she remained in awe of him and his Christian dedication to helping other people. For this reason it was difficult for her to imagine that she could possibly fall in love with him. Indeed, such an idea hardly occurred to her.

That Brian didn't express more clearly his deep, growing feelings for his young companion was later to cause him much grief. He had told the reporters at their press conference that he wasn't looking for a wife, but if he ever found that special woman he would marry her if she would have him. Well, he had found her, and quite by accident, but because Brian was an extremely busy man and because he knew that Lisa's emotions were not progressing as rapidly as his, he chose not to hurry her, but to enjoy each precious moment in her company, waiting until the time for their love was exactly right. How could he know that their right time might never come again?

One night in early summer Lisa was in the bathroom washing her hair when the telephone rang. She wrapped a large, fluffy towel securely about her dripping head and hurried to the bedroom to answer it. She smiled when Brian's clear, rich baritone came over the line.

"When did you get back?"

"I just came from the airport."

"How was your trip?"

"It was great! We were able to help some wonderful people back East. One case in particular brought joy to my heart. We found a six-year-old boy who, with the right operation, would be able to hear for the first time in his life, but there wasn't any chance for him because of the low income of his family. I wish you could have seen his face when he heard the birds chirping outside his window. And when he first heard the sound of his mother's voice it almost made me cry."

"Oh, Brian, that's so wonderful."

They went on talking along these lines, Brian sharing more of his experiences, especially the needs of Indians on nearby reservations, and Lisa bringing him up-to-date on the activities at her church and the latest happenings at Southern Pacific Airways.

"I'm having a kind of special get-together this weekend," Brian said then. "Elena starts work on her new film next week, and I thought I'd give a little party for her and some of the others working on the film. Will you come over and help me play host?"

If there had been a time a few short weeks earlier when Lisa would have been overwhelmed at the idea of attending a party with Hollywood celebrities, she thought little about it now. Through Brian and his active Christian life she had met countless persons from all walks of life, and most of them had turned out to be genuine and sincere in the efforts they pursued. In her almost childlike adoration of the philanthropist, she credited much of this to the scope of his influence, and she looked forward to meeting still more of those who made up the huge circle of his acquaintances.

"Sounds like fun."

"Shall I pick you up?"

"Why don't I just drive over? You'll have enough to do."

"Everyone will be staying the weekend, so pack a bag."

Saturday morning, dressed in khaki slacks and red blouse, Lisa loaded her suitcase into her Camaro and started for Brian's estate. The promise of a warm, cloud-free day lay in the vivid sky above, and when she pulled up before the immense wrought-iron gates they were thrown open in anticipation of expected guests. At the house Lisa parked behind several other cars, and as she climbed out with her suitcase she caught a glimpse of a Jaguar XKE parked a few yards away. She stopped a moment to admire its sleek white beauty. Peter had opened the door of the house and was crossing the veranda by the time she looked up.

"Morning, Lisa."

"Good morning, Peter—I was just admiring that beautiful sports car over there."

"That's Mr. Jeffery Stewart's car," he said, taking her piece of luggage. "He's the gentleman that's come over from London to direct Miss Elena's film"

Lisa and Peter entered the house together. "Where is our illustrious Mr. Sommervale this morning?" she asked.

"He's out by the pool with the guests, Lisa."

"Thank you, Peter."

Lisa left the foyer, walking past the sumptuous circular staircase and down the hall to the recreation room. She started to go outside, but froze suddenly in the open doorway. Striding across the patio was the most magnificent-looking man she had ever seen. He appeared to be in his early thirties, and he had a tall, slim build. His dark blonde hair, highlighted by the sun's bright glint, rippled softly in the breeze as he came toward her. He wore dark brown slacks and a creamy silk shirt. His handsome tanned face, like a great piece of sculpture, was shaped and molded in such absolute perfection that Lisa couldn't help staring at him. Eyes as blue as the vivid summer sky stared back with a look that went straight to her heart.

"Hello," the man said, offering her an enchanting white smile as he approached. "Are you looking for Brian?" He spoke with a strong British accent and his voice flowed from his perfect lips like soft velvet caressing a silken body on a cool night.

"Yes...I am."

"Well, he's—" The handsome Englishman turned to see Brian, in white slacks and blue print shirt, moving toward them through the gathering of people.

Brian's face lighted with a smile when he saw Lisa. He came to her side and placed an arm affectionately around her waist. "I was just coming to see if you'd arrived," he said, brushing her sunny cheek with a kiss. He glanced from Lisa to the Englishman. "I see you've met my favorite girl."

"Not formally," he replied, giving the tall, slender Lisa a silent appraisal. "But I hope you will take care of that right now."

"Lisa, I'd like you to meet Jeffery Stewart," Brian said. "Jeffery, this is Miss Lisa Palmer."

"How do you do, Miss Palmer?" the Englishman said, taking her hand firmly in his.

At his touch Lisa felt suddenly warmed, like the first rays of morning sunshine greeting the sparkling dew. "I'm pleased to meet you, Mr. Stewart."

"Jeffery," he said, and she felt her cheeks flame beneath another of his heart-deep gazes.

It was Heather's blatant intrusion upon the scene that hastily extinguished Lisa's glow and brought an end to the exciting tingle racing up and down her spine.

"Oh, Jeff, here you are," she called, approaching from the far end of the patio. "I wondered what had happened to you." She fastened her dark eyes on Lisa. "I'll thank you to let me have Jeff back!"

Lisa was about to utter a retort when Heather hooked her arm through Jeffery's saying, "Come on, darling, I want you to meet someone."

The magnificent Englishman turned his brilliant blue gaze fully on Lisa. "You'll excuse us?"

"Of course," she replied, and the handsome Jeffery Stewart strolled off across the patio with Heather fluttering attentively at his side.

Brian faced Lisa. "My sister's a little possessive of her new interest, isn't she?"

Lisa smiled. "A little, I think."

"Well, I hope she doesn't overdo it. Jeffery Stewart seems like a good man. Maybe Heather will get herself together at last."

Brian led Lisa around the patio, introducing her proudly to his guests—people from the film industry, and among them the popular actor Lance Whitworth. While Brian took care of his duties as host, Lisa talked at length with the tall, graying star and his lovely wife. But as the morning lingered on she found herself heeding the suave and charming Jeffery Stewart at every opportunity. Somehow he didn't seem as attentive to Heather as he could have been, and every time Lisa met his gaze a glow of pleasure stole through her.

In the afternoon, following an extravagant luncheon on the rear veranda overlooking the ocean, most of the guests changed into swimming attire and went down to the beach. One couple asked Brian and Elena to join them at the tennis courts, and a few others walked over to the stable.

Lisa and Maude donned swimsuits and sat sunning themselves by the circular pool. It was a bright, hot afternoon, with only a gentle breeze stirring the fronds of the palm trees. When footsteps sounded on the patio behind them, Maude turned to look up.

"Would you ladies care to join me for a swim?" Jeffery Stewart said in his smooth, velvet tone. He came up to them wearing brown-and-white striped trunks about his long, slim body.

"Shall we, Lisa?" Maude asked, and the Englishman held out a hand to each of them, appraising their appearance with a penetrating eye as they rose to their feet.

Lisa smiled up at him, his intense gaze giving her that same indescribable thrill as when they had first met.

The three of them walked to the edge of the pool and dived into the rippling face of the water. They swam its length several times before climbing out to sit on the edge as they dangled their feet in the clear water.

"Where's Heather?" Maude asked the Englishman.

"She went down to the beach."

"How did you manage to get away from her?"

Jeffery bestowed Brian's secretary with a striking, snow-white smile. "I told her I'd join her soon."

It was sooner than he expected.

"Well, Lisa, I see you've taken Jeff away from me again!" Heather proclaimed as she charged onto the patio from the direction of the beach.

"I was just on my way, darling," Jeffery said, rising to his feet.

"If you think you can tear yourself away!" Heather blazed.

Jeffery turned to Lisa. He winked and smiled. "Will you excuse us—again?"

There was a promise in that smile, Lisa thought, but she said with a reluctance she could barely conceal, "Of course. Have fun."

She watched them stroll the length of the patio and cross

the lawn to the beach, Heather clinging to Jeffery's arm with maternal possessiveness. *I don't blame you,* Lisa mused. *I'd cling to him too if I ever had the chance.*

"Jeffery is an attractive man, isn't he?" Maude observed.

"Don't you think that's putting it mildly?"

Brian's secretary regarded Lisa with a speculative gaze. She had little difficulty reading her thoughts. They were mirrored joyfully in the glow in her eyes and the smile on her lips.

"Forget it," Maude advised. "Heather already has a monopoly on him."

"That's what she thinks!" Lisa announced as she stood up.

"Where are you going?"

"Upstairs to dress for dinner."

"Already?"

"It may take me awhile," Lisa said, starting across the patio. Maude watched her go, a look of gentle amusement on her face.

For the formal dinner that evening Lisa had brought a floor-length gown. The dark green dress had white lace covering the top, and from the empire waist the long skirt flowed into a beautiful A-line. In the shower she shampooed her hair and then blew it dry with a hand dryer and set it on large electric rollers. While her hair was curling she manicured her nails and put forth a special effort in applying makeup to her classic, almost-perfect features. Then she brushed her shoulder-length blonde hair into curls at the back of her head. Among the curls she fastened a small green flower.

When at last she was ready to go downstairs she surveyed herself in the mirror on the closet door. There was no overbearing ego in Lisa's appraisal of her image, but she was sufficiently satisfied with her tall, slender looks, and while observing her reflection she wondered if Jeffery Stewart would take any special notice of her tonight. Could a man of his social stature and elegant taste take a real interest in a young woman of her background and manner? Probably not, she decided—she wouldn't be sophisticated or worldly enough for him.

A knock at the door jolted Lisa out of her thoughts, and she hurried to answer it. Brian let out a long, low whistle.

"You look ravishing."

"Why, thank you, kind sir," she said, exaggerating a bow.

Brian held out his arm. "Shall we join the others?"

In the living room Lisa cast a sweeping look over the throng of guests until she located Jeffery Stewart, handsome and tan, standing so tall above the gathering. And there was Heather perched beside him like a mother hen waiting for her nest of eggs to hatch.

When Peter came to the door announcing dinner, Lisa trouped along to the dining room with the others, hoping with all her heart to be seated next to the Englishman. But he was placed at one end of the table with Heather while she sat at the opposite end with Brian and Elena, and weighed in her mind the possibility of their host's sister having taken charge of the night's seating arrangement.

After dinner, dancing took place in the ballroom, with soft music provided by a splendid orchestra engaged for the evening's festivities. Lisa danced several dances with Brian as well as with Lance Whitworth and some of the other men before she walked out to the veranda and stood in the cool breeze gazing toward the moonlit beach. The circle of light from the dark, starry sky gave silver streaks to the gentle tide, and Lisa longed to share its peaceful, compelling beauty with Jeffery Stewart. But the last she had seen of him, he was whirling Heather around the dance floor, laughing into her upturned face and to all appearances falling completely under the spell she was trying to cast over him.

He walked quietly up behind her. "Would you care for some punch?"

Lisa thrilled at the sound of his voice and turned to accept the cup of fruit punch that Jeffery offered. "Thank you."

Jeffery wore a beautiful gray suit, the lapels of the coat trimmed in black velvet, and Lisa regarded with wonder the superlative good looks of the tall, blonde man at her side. In a moment she took a sip of the punch and smiled. "What have you done with Heather?"

"She's occupied with Lance for the moment."

"Maybe we'd better go back inside before she comes looking for you and creates a scene."

"Not yet," he said, taking her cup and setting it on a nearby table. "You must allow me at least one dance."

The soft, flowing music poured through the open doorway, filling the night air with a rhythmical enchantment as Jeffery took Lisa in his arms. His charm and gentleness engulfed her young heart, sending her thoughts reeling into a state of bliss unlike anything she had ever known. Soon the nearness of him caused her heart to pound with excitement in her throat.

"You look lovely tonight," he whispered, his vivid eyes pouring eagerly over the classic beauty of her face.

"Thank you," she mumured, a bewitching tingle rippling up and down her spine.

Jeffery examined her high cheekbones and tapering nose, his gaze lingering on her soft, wide mouth. How he yearned to place a kiss there. "I'm sorry we were interrupted this afternoon."

Even in high heels, Lisa had to look up at him. She smiled dreamily into his handsome face. "Heather can be insistent when she wants to."

They danced the length and breadth of the veranda again and again, their graceful silhouettes distinctly etched in the glow of moonlight streaming through the palm trees, and Lisa felt as if she had been born to fit into this man's arms.

When at last the gentle music came to a stop, she cast a prudent glance in the direction of the door.

"Later," he said as he clasped her hand and led her across

the luxuriant green of the lawn to the sandy earth of the beach, where they strolled along hand in hand for some time, relishing the moonlit night by the gentle shore. Lisa stole secret glances at the dashing Englishman and nestled her hand firmly in his, wishing with all her might that she could spend the rest of her days walking beside this man of fine appearance from the other side of the world.

At last Jeffery came to a stop and drew Lisa to him, wrapping her in a tender embrace. He gazed deeply into her up-turned face and then bent slowly and touched her waiting lips with a warm, moist kiss. How sweet and tender was his kiss, and how captivated was Lisa by his expression of deep, yearning passion!

It was when they started back to the house that she finally spoke. "Heather's probably looking all over for you."

"You let me worry about Heather," he said, closing an arm about her waist.

But when they reached the veranda Heather was just coming through the door. She stared at the two of them, coming toward her, arms linked. Lisa mentally braced herself for a distasteful scene, but to her acute surprise Heather merely brushed past her, pushing her aside, and snuggled up to the Englishman.

"Let's go for a drive, Jeff. I'm getting bored with Brian's little party. He doesn't even have anything to drink."

Jeffery glanced at Lisa, tossing her a look that said it would be easier for everyone if he did as Heather wanted. "All right, darling. See you later, Lisa."

As they turned and started around the house, Heather threw Lisa a backward, triumphant smile. Just as they disappeared from sight Maude stepped outside. Seeing the unhappy look on Lisa's face, she said, "What's wrong?"

"Oh, nothing really. It's just that Jeffery's gone off with Heather again."

"I told you she's taking all his time."

"Not all of it!" Lisa announced with a mischievous grin. She turned then and started for the door. "After I say good night to Brian, I'm going up to bed. See you in the morning."

※ ※ ※

Jeffery strode with an easy and refined motion along the silent corridor to his room. His thoughts were filled with his recent drive with Heather and some of what she had told him.

"You like Lisa a lot," she had accused, "but you're wasting your time with her. She's in love with my brother."

Jeffery didn't intend to take what Brian's sister had told him seriously. He had sensed he had stirred deep feelings in Lisa's heart, and he also knew that there were different kinds of love. It was quite obvious to anyone who cared to notice that Lisa plainly adored Brian Sommervale. But Jeffery was just as certain that she only considered the philanthropist a great friend.

The next morning Lisa woke early and had breakfast with Brian and Maude. She dressed for church later with a hopeful heart, half-expecting Jeffery to go with them, but as they prepared to leave he was sleeping soundly.

At the dinner table that afternoon, Lisa tried hard to arouse an interest in Livy's delicious meal, but her thoughts kept straying to Jeffery Stewart, and she found it difficult to keep from staring across the table at him.

Later in the day, after some of the guests had gone, those remaining gathered in the living room, where Brian sat down at the piano and filled the room with a glorious sound as his fingers glided expertly over the ivory keys. Much to Lisa's disappointment, she had little opportunity to talk with Jeffery throughout the day. Heather was never more than a few feet away from him, and shortly after Brian sat down at the piano they disappeared.

That evening when Lisa was getting ready to leave, Jeffery managed to disconnect himself from one of Heather's possessive grips long enough to find her and promise that he would give her a phone call very soon.

Chapter 8 ✿✿✿✿✿✿✿✿✿✿✿✿✿

Monday night when Lisa got home from her job at Southern Pacific Airways, she called Sue to tell her about the exciting and wonderful man she had met over the weekend.

"He's the most magnificent-looking man I've ever seen. I couldn't believe my eyes when I first saw him. And he's so charming and sophisticated."

"He sounds too good to be true," said Sue. "I can't wait to meet him. If he's better-looking than Brian Sommervale—"

"I think he must be everything," Lisa confided. "He said he'd call me, so I'll let you know what happens."

Throughout the week Lisa anxiously awaited Jeffery's promised call. She daydreamed about what he might say to her in his beautiful velvet voice, and how he would ask her for a date. She thought about all the interesting places he might take her, and her excitement and anticipation grew with each passing day. So enthralled with this man was Lisa that, instead of staying late at Southern Pacific to get in some air work as she often did, she rushed home from her job every evening to wait by the telephone for the call she knew would come.

When Saturday arrived and Jeffery had not telephoned, she began to worry. But when she paused to think the situation over, she marveled at how quickly she had become smitten with a man she scarcely knew. She told herself that she was being foolish—that never before had anyone, with the exception of Brian, had such an overwhelming effect on her. And even the great awe and admiration she had for the humanitarian couldn't touch the fresh and growing emotions she felt for Jeffery Stewart. He said he would call soon, but he was involved with Elena's film, and how many other women were awaiting a call from him? How many wouldn't even wait, but would seek him out on their own? Would Heather?

If he didn't call, so what, Lisa decided. It wasn't as if the end of the world had come. Not quite.

That afternoon when the telephone rang out in her tiny bungalow, Lisa ran to answer it, positive that Jeffery's beautiful, fluent voice would be at the other end of the line.

"Oh, Brian."

"What do you mean, 'Oh, Brian'? You sound sorry that I called."

"No. It's nothing. How are you?"

"I'm doing great, but obviously you're not. What's wrong, Lisa?"

"Nothing."

"What are you doing?"

"Not much of anything."

"What have you been doing this week?"

"Working."

When she didn't elaborate, Brian cleared his throat and said, "You didn't have to answer the phone."

She laughed. "I'm sorry. I don't mean to be so... whatever."

"You sound like you could do with some cheering up. I'll come over about eight and we'll go somewhere for dinner."

Lisa hesitated, not wanting to say no to her beloved friend, but hating to go out in case Jeffery should call. Finally she said, "Let's make it another time, Brian. I think I'll stay home and get lost in a good book tonight."

"Hey, what is this? Are you trying to get rid of me?"

"Of course not."

"Then why do I get the distinct impression that you want me to get lost?"

"You know better than that. It's just that...well, I was expecting someone else."

"Oh? Anyone I know?"

"As a matter of fact, it's Jeffery Stewart."

Brian pictured Lisa's lovely face in his mind. He could see her radiant green eyes, swirling, compelling before him like the beautiful, timeless sea. His heart ached just at the thought of her.

"You and Heather," was all he could say, and even then his voice sounded like an empty hollow in his ears.

"I know. Is she...is she spending a lot of time with him?"

"I really don't know. You know how I'm gone so much. And my sister doesn't discuss her personal affairs much with me anymore. But that's why I wanted to see you tonight. I'm leaving town again tomorrow afternoon. I'll be gone a couple weeks. But I'll call you when I get back."

They said good-bye and Lisa sat on the couch feeling a little apprehensive. Brian hadn't sounded pleased that she was hoping for a call from Jeffery. But she couldn't expect him to be happy that she was interested in the same man his sister wanted. And Heather had evidently made up her mind she was going to have Jeffery for herself, if her actions of the previous weekend were any indication of how she felt. Lisa thought about this for awhile, wondering if Jeffery Stewart hadn't called her because he had been busy with Elena's film and perhaps other dates, or if he had been busy courting Brian's troubled sister.

Sunday after church Lisa spent a gloomy afternoon in her house waiting for the phone to ring. When it did not, she resolved that the Englishman had no intention of calling her—that he had probably just been playing a game. He was much inclined toward the pleasures of the world, Lisa told herself, and she began to wonder why she felt so drawn to a man who lived in such contrast to the values that she had in life.

The next week Lisa tried to dismiss Jeffery Stewart totally from her mind. When his promised call did not come, she decided that perhaps it was for the best. Yet as the days dragged along, the supremely handsome Englishman was ever-present in Lisa's thoughts. She remembered the thrill of his touch, the hunger in his kiss, the approving look in his eyes. She remembered until she could think of little else.

Then finally, on the following Saturday morning, when she had all but lost hope of ever hearing from Jeffery Stewart, her much-longed-for call came.

Lisa dressed with special care for her date that night. In his beautiful flowing voice, Jeffery had apologized for calling her on such short notice, explaining how tied up he had been with Elena's film. When he asked Lisa to have dinner with him, she could scarcely believe she was actually going to see him again.

"Hello," he said when Lisa had opened the door. He looked her up and down, assuring her even though silent in his approval.

She had chosen to wear a soft, flowing dress of crepe de chine with a camisole-style bodice and open coat. With her black-and-white dress she wore black patent high-heeled sandals and white gold accessories.

To Lisa the two short weeks since she had seen Jeffery seemed like an eternity, and as she stood in her doorway gazing up at him, she examined him prudently as if to reassure herself that he was just as she remembered—so tall and lean and graceful, with hair dark blonde and brilliant blue eyes. Most of all, there before her discerning gaze was his handsome, tanned face, like a great piece of sculpture, shaped and molded in absolute perfection.

At a quiet inn along the beach, the waiter seated them at a table in the corner of a dimly lit and cozy room. The sound of gentle waves rushing over the shore and soft music coming from the band in an adjoining room added to the atmosphere of relaxed enjoyment as they had a scrumptious dinner, laughing and talking animatedly while they ate. Lisa asked Jeffery about his film, and this led to talk of Elena and Lance Whitworth.

"Lance is happily married, of course," Jeffery said, "a miracle in this crazy business."

"Elena's never been married, has she?"

"No, but give her time. She's only a few years older than you are and she's an intelligent woman—not one to rush into anything like that. She's cautious about everything now."

"She and Brian both say they're nothing more than friends, but I wonder if there's really more to it than that. They seem to have something pretty special between them."

"It's special all right," Jeffery said, "but it's not what you think. Brian befriended Elena at a time when she didn't think she had a friend left. At the beginning of her career she got mixed up with some unpleasant characters and got into drugs through them—cocaine. There was a lot of publicity about it several years ago, but it's all died away now."

"I might have known. I think the basis for every relationship Brian has is the fact that he's done something for the other person. Even Maude. Livy told me that Maude was going through a terrible experience with a man several years ago. She even tried to commit suicide. But Brian heard about her trouble, and even though she's older than he is, he took her under his wing and gave her life new meaning."

"That seems to be Brian's way," Jeffery observed. "With everyone except you. The basis for his relationship with you is just the opposite."

Lisa smiled across the table at him. "Yes, it is. I hadn't thought of that before."

Later when they left the restaurant Jeffery offered Lisa his arm. "Shall we go for a walk?"

They crossed the parking lot and traversed a narrow path that led to the wide sandy beach. The night was clear, with dazzling stars dotting the black sky and a balmy breeze blowing the fine sand beneath their feet. Jeffery took Lisa's hand in his and they strolled aimlessly along the deserted shore, their long silhouettes etched against the backdrop of lazily rushing water.

Lisa gazed up at the good-looking Englishman, thinking how wonderful it was to be with him again. It was as though she hadn't really been alive until the two weeks before when Brian had introduced them, and this evening with him had convinced her that she wanted to spend as much time with him as possible.

They ambled along without speaking for awhile until Jeffery's velvet tone broke in on the lull of the night. "I couldn't have dreamed a lovelier night or a more charming lady to spend it with."

They stopped walking and Lisa cast radiant eyes upon his magnificent face. He pulled her near and bent to kiss her eagerly on the mouth. A tingle of excitement tore through her as his soft lips touched hers and she warmly returned his strong expression of affection.

Jeffery could feel the vibrations coming from the slender woman in his arms, which increased his desire for her, but at the same time he sensed another feeling—a feeling he found lacking in other encounters. When he released her, she looked up sweetly at him and he stared deeply into the glow of her lovely emerald eyes, thinking how unlike other women she seemed. She was pure and untried, he thought, like a fine misty rain in the English springtime.

He slid his arm around her waist and they started back toward the inn.

"I want to apologize again for not calling you," he said. "I've been so busy with this film that I haven't taken time for anything, not even a phone call."

"Your work must be very demanding," she said, feeling a little guilty for assuming that he had been spending time with Heather.

"But the pay is good."

They laughed and Lisa said, "How many films do you direct a year?"

"I do two or three."

"Do you have a favorite one?"

"I've enjoyed them all. I get a certain feeling about a film when I read the script. I can feel if it's right for me. And I've set a standard for myself. Some kinds of films I just won't do, not for any amount of money."

"Good for you!"

"How's your business? Brian mentioned that you work for a regional airline."

"We've had good flying weather recently, so business has been even better than usual."

"And you're interested in flying yourself. Do you make any flights for your company?"

"No. I'm not qualified—not yet. I'd have to get my commercial license and instrument rating first. Right now I just fly for my own pleasure in the Bonanza, but Jerry's been instructing me in the Aztec and Cessna when he has time." She flicked her gaze up at him. "Would you like to go up sometime?"

"Of course. As long as Brian does the flying."

"Thanks for the confidence," she replied in her soft drawl.

"I was joking," Jeffery said with a laugh. "I'll go up with you. I'll let you know when I've worked up enough nerve."

She glanced up at him again. He was smiling his charming white smile.

"A Bonanza is a single-engine plane, isn't it?" he asked in a minute.

"Yes."

"What do you do in a single-engine plane when the engine konks out?"

"During the initial climb or at cruise?"

"Anytime."

"It's never happened to me, but it might. The best preparation is prevention. Vic, one of my bosses, is one of the best aircraft men around, so I'm quite confident flying his plane, but if it does happen, the worst time is during the intial climb, the time between liftoff to the first power reduction. This is when things are happening and changing quickly."

"What about when you're just cruising along, say you're up a few thousand feet and all of a sudden—nothing?"

"If you were up about seven or eight thousand feet in a single-engine plane, you'd have about ten minutes' time and about 12 miles or so of range in any direction. Of course the range would be affected by the wind—you'd have more than 12 miles with the wind at the tail and less if the plane is heading into it. But there's no reason to panic, since a light airplane will glide to the ground, and usually a safe place to land can be found in plenty of time."

"Sounds like you know what you're talking about. I guess it'll be safe to put my life in your hands."

Lisa laughed. "Of course it's safe."

When they reached the inn's parking lot and Jeffery's Jaguar, Lisa walked around the car admiring it slowly.

"Would you like to drive it?" he asked, taking pleasure in her obvious interest.

After only a minute's hesitation, Lisa went around to the driver's side and Jeffery climbed in the passenger's seat and leaned over to open the door for her. She slid beneath the wheel and took the keys from him. Soon they were racing along the coast highway.

"It has a lot of power, doesn't it?" she asked, enthralled by the beauty and efficiency of the sports car. "How fast will it go?"

"It'll do about 140."

"You don't need that much power," she reasoned in typical feminine fashion. "How big is the engine?"

"It's a 5.3-liter V-12."

She threw him an uncertain glance. "Maybe you'd better drive after all."

He laughed at her and then they fell silent for a time.

"Tell me more about your work," she said presently. "Do you work mostly in London?"

"Yes. But I've done films all over—France, Italy, Spain."

"What will you do when you finish Elena's film?" she further questioned him, sounding not exceptionally interested.

"I've been approached to do another film here when I finish this one."

Lisa focused her attention on the road ahead, not daring to hope that he would stay in Los Angeles for any length of time.

"Would you like for me to stay?"

Taken unaware by his question, she glanced quickly at him in frustration for the proper reply. Finally she answered in the only way she knew how—honestly. "Yes, I'd like that very much."

At her cottage Lisa invited Jeffery in for coffee. She swept a hand toward the brown couches on her way to the kitchen. "Sit down, I'll only be a minute."

Jeffery joined her in the kitchen a short time later. "Your place is nice, but is this all of it?"

"You sound like Brian," she said, reaching into a nearby cabinet for a ceramic tray. She placed a small matching coffee service and two cups on the tray.

He took it back to the living room and they sat side by side on the couch drinking the coffee and talking quietly. At last Jeffrey set his cup on the table and stood up.

"I'd better be going. Thank you for the coffee. And the company."

"You're welcome," she said, going with him to the door.

"I'll call you tomorrow."

When he took her in his arms, kissing her hungrily, her response was eager and natural, and in that instant Lisa knew that Jeffery Stewart had kindled a flame deep inside her—a flame she believed was destined to burn forever.

Chapter 9 ❀❀❀❀❀❀❀❀❀❀❀

*T*he next afternoon when Jeffery picked up Lisa, they went for a drive along the coast and then stopped for dinner at a small, out-of-the-way restaurant. After the meal they drove to a peaceful spot on the beach, where they trod along hand in hand as they had the night before, talking and laughing as they went. When they returned to the car, the blazing sun was just dropping like a huge fiery ball in the distant sky.

They faced each other beside the car, arms entwined, and Lisa gazed deeply into the infinite blue of Jeffery's eyes, wondering about this man to whom she was so ready to commit her heart.

"What do you see when you look at me that way?" he said, at last breaking the spell.

"I don't know. I was just thinking, I guess. I was just thinking how good God has been to send a man like you into my life."

"Maybe it wasn't God, but the devil," he teased.

"No. Everything good comes from God."

And what if it only seems good, thought Jeffery.

In the upcoming weeks Jeffery was busy at the studio, but as the days went by he found he wanted to be with Lisa more and more. He was captivated by her openness and sincerity and by her loveliness and vitality. He perceived a difference

93

in her and was lured by it. They spent their free hours getting better acquainted and enjoying the endless pleasures of the surrounding environment.

One Sunday afternoon shortly after Lisa returned from church the telephone rang. She was in the bedroom changing clothes, so reached for the phone on the table beside the bed.

"Good morning," Jeffery said.

"It's good afternoon, and you sound like you're still asleep."

"I just woke up. The first person I thought of was you, and I couldn't wait to hear the sound of your husky little Southern voice."

"Hey, that's my line."

"Why?"

"Because your voice is the most beautiful sound I've ever heard. I think it must have been borrowed from an angel. A distinctly British angel, of course."

Jeffery chuckled. "I don't think I can quite handle those lofty heights, not even British ones, but I'm glad it pleases you."

"It pleases me, but the sound of your voice isn't enough. I want to see your face too."

"What would you like to do while you're looking at it?"

"That alone is enough to last me a lifetime."

Jeffery laughed softly in her ear again.

"I mean it. You must know how handsome you are."

"Not me. I've been looking at this face in the mirror every day for as long as I can remember. It's just a face to me."

"That's a beautiful attitude. I don't know which is more beautiful, your attitude or your face. I'll have to think about it."

"What do you want to do while you're thinking about it?"

"Anything you want to do is fine with me."

"Do you like the mountains?"

"Yes."

"Why don't I pick you up about two? We can eat somewhee on the way."

Lisa's excitement grew as she changed from the two-piece dress she had worn to church into tailored slacks and ruffled blouse. She freshened her makeup at the bathroom mirror and brushed her golden hair till it glistened brightly. When the doorbell chimed her heart banged crazily against her ribs and funny little shivers chased each other through her body. She opened the door and stared at Jeffery standing so tall before her. How splendid he looked in gray slacks and matching sweater!

"I like your hair down on your shoulders that way, darling," he said, and kissed her affectionately on the mouth. Then he gave her a small box tied with a yellow ribbon.

Lisa unwrapped the package to find a box of assorted chocolates. She took off the lid. "Umm, they look delicious. Thank you." she offered him the box.

"I'm starved," he said, taking several pieces of the rich confection.

"Let me cook you something before we go."

"We'll get something on the way."

"I'm all ready, but are you sure I can't cook you some breakfast?"

"It's time for lunch now."

She smiled up at him, then helped herself to a piece of candy and laid the box on the coffee table and picked up her purse. He followed her outside and closed the door behind them.

They had a quiet lunch at a restaurant in Oceanview, and afterward drove the short distance to the base of the mountains. As they started up the high terrain, the landscaping was thick and green with massive trees pointing their full heads toward the thinly scattered clouds. Gradually while climbing the air became cooler, and Jeffery stopped the car along the winding road and put up the convertible top.

"It's all so beautiful, isn't it?" Lisa said when they started up again. She gazed solemnly out the window. "It's amazing what God can do. I haven't been up here much lately. Since I met Brian, I've spent most of my spare time with him."

"You have?"

Lisa turned to study her attractive companion, wondering if she detected a hint of jealousy in his question. It made her feel good to think that he might care enough to be even partly jealous of Brian.

"He's been a wonderful friend to me," she said in a minute.

"But that's all?"

"Yes, that's all," she replied with a smug little grin.

They drove deeper into the mountains, taking delight in the well-defined difference in climate and scenery. After awhile they stopped at a lookout point and got out of the car. In the cool, refreshing air the widespread view of green valleys and hillsides was astounding. Lisa nestled close to Jeffrey on the edge of the cliff, marveling at the panoramic sight before them. Enraptured in the warmth and security of his arms, she was willing to stay indefinitely in his protective bosom while the fast-paced world around them went racing by. But the touch of his sweet lips on hers brought her joyfully back to reality and the day that lay ahead.

They resumed their drive, and as afternoon grew into evening, Jeffery slowed his car to a stop in front of a big cabin structure. The sign hanging between two posts read Mountain Springs Restaurant.

"Ooh, it's really chilly now that the sun isn't shining," Lisa commented as they climbed out of the Jaguar. "I forgot to bring a jacket."

Jeffery smiled down on her and pulled her close, warming her with the nearness of his firm, lean body. They entered the restaurant like that, arms around each other's waist.

Inside it was warm and comfortable. A huge rock fireplace, with yellow-and-red flames crackling in the hearth, ran along one wall, and a wooden bar covered the length of another. Several couples were seated at the wooden tables and chairs that filled the expansive dining room. Jeffery led Lisa to a table in front of a vast window that framed an enormous view of the mountain peaks and valleys. But during the meal they seemed little interested in the beauty outside. Their eyes met and held across the table, and the world around them seemed to fade away. Lisa placed her hand on the checkered table-cloth; Jeffery closed his own hand over hers and thrilled her with tender glances. What was it in his sheer touch that said it all, she wondered. Why this man rather than any other? Heaven alone knew the answer, but as sure as there was an answer Lisa knew she was falling deeply in love with Jeffery Stewart.

Darkness covered them when they at last left the restaurant and started back down the mountain.

"Have you heard from Heather lately?" she asked as they rode along.

"She's called me a few times."

"I can't help thinking about her."

"Do you have a guilty conscience, darling?"

She glanced over at him. "Whatever do you mean?"

"All's fair in love and war."

"Jeffery!" she cried in outrageous indignation.

He smiled into her lovely blazing eyes. "You did take me away from her."

"I didn't do any such thing!"

"I was seeing her before I met you. *But* I was rapidly losing interest."

"You're free to spend your time with whomever you please." She delivered this with an indifferent shrug.

"And it pleases me to spend it with you," he replied, reaching for her.

She nestled beside him with his arm around her shoulders. "I feel sorry for Heather and little Eric. I wish I could do something to help."

"I don't think Heather wants any help, darling. She's the self-destructive kind. With people like her there isn't anything you can do except sit back and watch."

"Maybe you could help her. She probably cares a great deal for you."

"She may think she does, but Heather is still in love with her dead husband. She's running away from what happened, and she may keep running until she winds up like he did."

"Oh, Jeffery, I hope not. Poor Eric. It seems like he would be a compensation to Heather for her loss."

"She doesn't seem to care very much about anyone, especially herself." He sent her a measured look. "She told me on the night of Brian's party that you were in love with her brother."

"She's always thought I was out to get Brian, or get something from him, but—"

"But you're really out to get me, am I right?"

She smiled innocently at him.

"You didn't answer my question, darling."

"I'm not going to. And that's called evading the issue."

"It's also called as good as pleading guilty."

"Sometimes," she smugly agreed.

When they returned to the foot of the mountains, Jeffery drove along till they came to the Coast Highway. He parked the car at a secluded section of beach and put the top down.

"Smell that ocean," he said, taking a deep breath of salty air. "The mountains are nice, but this is the best of all."

"When you're here it is," she said, her emerald eyes bright with adoration.

He slid his arm around her, and they sat quietly watching

the surf lap at the edge of the land. "I've enjoyed this day so much," he said.

"I have too. It's so good just being with you."

Gently he took her in his arms and kissed her, and Lisa felt as if the whole world were right there in that little car on that lonely stretch of beach.

Chapter 10 ✸✸✸✸✸✸✸✸✸✸

The next week was a hard working one for Jeffery. He put in long hours at the studio, but each night he called Lisa before he went to bed. She kept busy with her job, but lived only for the time when they could be together. Late on Friday afternoon the telephone on her desk summoned Lisa from the filing cabinet.

"Good afternoon, Southern Pacific Airways."

"Good afternoon," said a smooth, velvet voice. "I hope I'm not disturbing you, but I had a few minutes and I wanted to call and tell you that we'll probably wind things up early tonight. I'd like to see you."

"I'd like to see you too," she said, her voice rising with the excitement she felt.

"Where would you like to go?"

"I don't know—anywhere. I know—why don't I cook dinner? I've never cooked for you, and I love to experiment around in the kitchen."

"I'll be your guinea pig anytime, darling."

She laughed into the phone. "It won't be that bad."

"I'll see you tonight, darling."

Lisa had finished work and was about to leave the office when Vic came in the back door. "It's going to be a great night for flying," he said. "The Bonanza's all ready to go."

She came around the desk with her purse in her hand. "Not tonight, Vic."

"What's this?"

"I can't tonight. I'm going to be busy."

"You've been busy a lot lately." Vic smiled mischievously. "Okay, kid, what's his name?"

She laughed. "How'd you know?"

"You don't usually let anything keep you out of an airplane. It has to be a man."

"His name is Jeffery Stewart. And he's very special."

"Well, good luck, kid."

She started for the door. "See you Monday."

"Yeah, see you. Hey," he called after her, "bring him around sometime. Does he like to fly?"

"He's going up with me sometime," she said over her shoulder.

Lisa made two stops on her way home. The first one was at the supermarket in Oceanview Shopping Center. She bought two thickly-cut steaks, a carton of sour cream, a package of dinner rolls, and fresh vegetables for salad. Then she drove to Sue and Mark's house.

"You can stay and eat with us," Sue greeted. "I was just starting dinner."

"Thanks, but I can only stay a minute," Lisa said. "I just came by to borrow your card table."

"I'll get it for you," Mark said from the kitchen doorway, then disappeared down the hall.

"How've you been?" Sue asked. "We don't see much of you anymore."

"I've been doing just fine. How about you two?"

"We've been doing fine too," Sue said a little impatiently. Then she smiled. "Now quit beating around the bush and tell me how things are going with you and Jeffery."

"I really believe this is it for me," Lisa said. "I've never felt this way about any other man. Jeffery's so wonderful, and when we're together I feel like it was meant to be from the beginning of time.''

Sue examined her friend's dreamy expression. ''You're pretty sure about all this? You're really in love with him?''

''Yes, I am. And I think he's falling in love with me too.''

''I guess I was wrong, then,'' said Sue. ''I thought for sure it would be you and Brian Sommervale.''

Lisa shook her blonde head. ''Sue, he's just a friend. I guess he's about the most beautiful and special friend I've ever had, but I don't love him the way I love Jeffery. And of course Brian's not looking for a wife. He's so dedicated to his work. My goodness, can you believe my life now? I used to be just a little old nobody who never did anything really special—''

''Until you saved the life of a millionaire philanthropist.''

''And then he introduced me to the famous film director, Jeffery Stewart. I don't know what to think anymore. Why, anything can happen!''

''Lisa, everyone knows how genuine Brian Sommervale is, but I'm not so sure about your Jeffery Stewart.''

''Why do you say that?''

''I don't know. It's just a silly feeling I've had ever since you first told me about him. I've heard of his reputation as a director and I've seen some of his films. He's magnificent. But what do you really know about him personally?''

''I know he's wonderful, Sue. And I know I love him with all my heart.''

Sue smiled then. ''Well, I'm sure glad for you. I wish you all the happiness in the world. Be sure and invite me to the wedding.''

''Oh, I'll want you to be in it. You and my sister.''

Mark came back with the card table under one arm.

''Oh, thanks, Mark,'' Lisa said. ''I want to borrow this because Jeffery's coming to dinner tonight.''

''Why do you need this?'' Mark asked. ''You've got a table in your kitchen.''

"I thought I'd fix a table in the living room, and this will be easier to handle. I want our dinner to be romantic, with candles and soft music and everything. You know, just the right atmosphere."

"You're really setting this guy up for the kill, aren't you?" Mark asked.

They all laughed as they walked out to Lisa's car and Mark put the card table in the trunk.

"Bring Jeffrey over sometime," Sue said as Lisa got in behind the wheel. "I'm dying to meet this irresistible hunk."

"I will," Lisa promised with a laugh. After a few more parting words she was off.

❋　❋　❋

The next afternoon Lisa was getting ready to go out and do her shopping when the doorbell chimed. She came from the bedroom to answer it.

"Miss Lisa Palmer?" spoke a heavyset man in a green uniform. He was holding a long white box under his arm.

"Yes."

"Sunset Florist. Will you sign here, please?" he said, thrusting out a slip of paper and a pen.

She wrote her name on the paper and returned it to the man. "Thank you," she said, and took the box. As he left she walked over to the couch and sat down. Then she untied the bright red ribbon on the box and excitedly lifted the lid.

"Oh, my goodness!" she cried at the sight of the long-stemmed red roses nestled inside. She took one of the flowers in her hand and inhaled its lovely fragrance. In a minute she replaced the rose alongside the others and picked up the enclosed card, smiling at the sweet note that Jeffery had written:

> Thank you for sharing a lovely evening with me,
>
> Your Jeffery

Your Jeffery. Could it be that one day soon he would really be hers? Was he growing to love her as much as she loved him? And would he soon ask her to become his wife?

Lisa held the card tenderly to her breast for a long moment before going to place it inside her little white Bible on the dresser in the bedroom. Then, after arranging the roses in a vase on the coffee table, she began dressing to go out, thinking about her actions of the previous night.

She had sensed the moment Jeffery had entered her living room and taken her in his arms that she might have made a mistake in preparing such a romantic dinner for them at her cottage. The candlelight. The soft music. The nearness of their bodies as they danced. It had been too much for both of them. But Jeffery had accepted her refusals of his ardor with good grace, saying good night at the door with a gentle kiss and a promise to see her tonight. Perhaps she was being foolish, Lisa thought, to stick so rigidly to her Christian convictions concerning her relationship with Jeffery. After all, times were different now, and making love with a man at the slightest proposal was the accepted thing. How many women would gladly trade places with her? How many would eagerly seek a physical association with him?

But she couldn't be something she was not. And to regard love as incidental was impossible for her—not that what she felt for Jeffery even approached the casual. And that was what troubled her. He was a persuasive man, and every day she was growing more in love with his calm nature, his elegant charm and sophistication. Every day it seemed harder to resist his gentle demands. But why should she really, if they were to be married? And if he loved her they soon would be. But did she truly want that kind of relationship with him before they became husband and wife? She knew she did not—that for her the only right commitment was a permanent one vowed before God and all who cared to witness it.

That night when Jeffery came to pick her up, Lisa was

waiting for him in a black dress with wrist-length sleeves of black lace. She wore matching hosiery and high-heeled sandals, and in her long hair she had fastened a sparkling pin.

Jeffery, in dark suit and tie, greeted her eagerly and tenderly. "You're lovely," he murmured, taking her in his arms for a lasting kiss. In his deep embrace her love for him filled her utterly, and she believed that never again could she know such magnitude of emotion.

"Thank you for the roses. They're beautiful," she said when he finally released her.

"They serve only to grace the beauty already here."

"Why, thank you, kind sir," she said smiling up into his handsome face.

He pulled her to him again, touching his lips to her soft golden hair and whispering words of sweet endearment. But when she lifted her gaze to his, Lisa was puzzled by what she saw. His perfect lips wore a smile, but the expression in his bold eyes seemed sad and desperate.

They had dinner at an exclusive restaurant and went to the theater afterward. Later they drove back to her cottage, and as soon as they were seated on the couch, he drew her near, kissing and caressing her expertly. His expressions of affection came easily at first, but gradually he became more ardent. Soon Lisa was a glowing flame in his arms. His lips were soft and moist upon hers, and his touch was strong but controlled. When she felt their emotions beginning to soar, she persuaded him to go for a walk on the beach. The chilly air quickly calmed their fiery excitement, and when they returned to the house he prepared to say good night to her at the door.

"I must go, darling, it's very late."

She gazed dreamily up at him, not yet wanting to say good night but knowing it could be her undoing if she invited him in again. Instead she turned her thoughts in another direction, toward something she had been wanting to ask Jeffery since they had first begun dating.

"Jeffery, I'm not sure if this is exactly the right time, but—"

"I only know of one way to find out."

Lisa was uncertain about how to approach him on a subject so dear to her heart. She knew Jeffery was not a religious man—at least he had given no indication of it when she talked of its importance in her life. But she had not let this matter dampen their relationship. She had been too caught up in her attraction to this man, too busy falling madly in love with him. But now what mattered most in her life was surfacing again, and she wanted Jeffery to be a part of it.

"I was...I was wondering if...if you would go to church with me sometime?" she said, her words pouring out hesitantly, brokenly, as if she had given them little thought.

Jeffery glared at her, a look of incredulity on his striking features. Only a short time ago she had driven him to the brink of emotion, and now she wanted to talk about church! Gazing into her upturned face, so trusting and full of expectation, he thought about this young woman who was fast becoming such a significant part of his life. It was the little things about her that told him so much—her comments about her proper upbringing, her regular church attendance, her profound admiration for Brian Sommervale and his dedicated work. Lisa was so different from the kind of women he knew, and sometimes he wondered why he bothered with her. Maybe in the back of his mind he knew, and now with this ridiculous question of hers about church he would have to lay some of his feelings on the line—a thing he hadn't done in a long time. Perhaps he had *never* done it. Lisa's question, while meaning little to the indifferent Jeffery Stewart, was of supreme importance to her, and as he sensed this he offered a response that he hoped sounded sincere.

"Of course I'll go, darling."

"Tomorrow is Sunday—will you go then?"

How could he say no to that earnest plea in her lovely eyes? "Does it mean so much to you?"

"Very much."

He paused, laughing at himself. "Yes, I'll go," he said at last, and silently he questioned the presence of his sanity.

When they left the churchyard and drove to a nearby restaurant, a warm, bright afternoon lay joyfully before them, but Lisa couldn't quite get caught up in the mood. The minister's sermon that morning had been on God's plan of salvation, and she had stolen secret glances at Jeffery while listening to the life-giving words, wondering if he had ever given any thought to the matter of his soul. And though it had felt good to be in the Lord's house with the man He had surely sent for her to love, it troubled her deeply to think that he might not be saved.

At dinner Jeffrey brought up the subject that had been on her mind for most of the morning.

"Religion's never been a very important part of my life, as it has yours."

"Why not?" When he only shrugged, she said, "What *is* important to you?"

"My work, I suppose."

"What do you believe in?"

"I believe in myself."

"You should. You have a lot going for you, but have you ever thought that everything good you have is a gift from God?" His look of unconcern prompted her to go on. "You do believe in God, don't you, Jeffery?"

"I've never doubted."

"But that's only intellectual knowledge. You have to believe with your heart."

"I've never felt any need of that kind. I haven't thought about it."

"You're a kind and good man, Jeffery. The only true comparison is to Jesus, who was supremely good."

"I wouldn't try to compete with Him or with your belief in Him."

"Belief in his life, death, and resurrection gives you eternal life."

Jeffery shook his dark blonde head absently. "I don't need your Jesus, but if He makes you happy that's all right with me."

Lisa felt something like a stab of pain strike in the pit of her stomach, and in her heart she felt a deep, aching throb. For the first time she allowed herself the full realization that she had fallen in love with a man who did not know or love God. And as much as this hurt her, as much as she longed for Jeffery to share her faith in Him, she knew this was something she could not push. She could only respect his feelings, acknowledge her own faith, and pray that one day he would feel his need.

Chapter 11 *********

Some of California's loveliest countryside lay to the north of Oceanview. When Lisa and Jeffery left the restaurant they drove around most of the afternoon enjoying the sights—tall oak trees, vast green farmlands, and spreading grape vineyards. They had passed several roadside stands arrayed with fresh fruits and vegetables of every taste and color when Lisa glanced over at Jeffery.

"Tell me something about England."

Jeffery's great love for his homeland lighted excitement and joy in his handsome face as he spoke, and his smooth, velvet voice grew husky with emotion. "It's the most beautiful country you've ever seen. It's so green it almost hurts your eyes to look at it." He took his gaze from the road to look briefly at her. "It's even greener than your eyes."

"Are you from London?"

"I grew up there, but I was born in Brighton. It's on the coast of the English Channel, about 50 miles from London."

"Tell me about all the places I've heard so much about. Like Scotland Yard. In movies and stories the policemen are usually portrayed as being so inept, but I'll bet they aren't like that at all."

"Most of them are dedicated men who work very hard. Scotland Yard itself is a street between Whitehall and the Victoria Embankment. The building sits on land once owned by Scotland.''

''Tell me about the Tower of London where the Crown Jewels are kept.''

''They're in an underground jewel house. The tower is actually several buildings. It was once a palace and later a prison. You probably know that Anne Boleyn was executed there.''

She nodded and said, ''Some of the streets of London are as famous as the buildings, aren't they? Downing Street has always sounded so alluring to me.''

''It's just an ordinary short street. Whitehall is at one end and St. James Park is at the other. Number Ten Downing Street is the prime minister's home. Oxford and Picadilly streets are some of the shopping areas of London. I think you would like Kings Road in Chelsea.''

''Jeffery, it all sounds so wonderful—places I've heard of, like Hyde Park, Westminster Abbey and the Houses of Parliament, and of course Big Ben. But tell me what the people are like. You British subjects—isn't that what you're called? What kinds of things do you do? Where do you go, for instance?''

''Wait a minute!'' he laughed. ''You're getting ahead of me. We're like people everywhere, I suppose. We get up in the morning and go to work. We shop. We go out at night to the casinos and restaurants and operas—''

''And to the pubs and discoteques,'' she added.

''Something is always going on in London. There are so many ceremonial events at the historical buildings and parks. Londoners get out and do things. We're active and patriotic.''

''British subjects don't sound so very different from American citizens.''

''Ah, but we do have some differences. And by the way, do you know why we are called British subjects?''

''Of course. Great Britain is historically a monarchy. What

are some of those differences you mentioned?"

"All right. How about this? You wear a raincoat, but I wear an oilskin. And you carry packages and eat potato chips. I carry parcels and eat crisps."

"I know one. I eat baked potatoes and you eat potatoes in their jackets. Why are you Britons so formal about everything?"

He laughed and said, "How about this? On a dark night you might use a flashlight, but I'd use a pocket torch."

Lisa giggled. "You better be careful, you might catch your pocket on fire."

"Your sense of humor is a little different from mine too, darling," he said, and they both laughed again. "If you called me in London it would be a long-distance call, but if I called you from there it would be a trunk call."

"And you call an apartment a flat."

"And a flat is a puncture. A divided highway is a dual carriageway. And we don't pass cars in England—we overtake them."

"You know what?" Lisa said excitedly. "I'd love to see London! And Brighton, because you were born there. Will you take me there sometime? Will you take me to see all of England?"

When Jeffery didn't answer, she glanced curiously at him. In a minute she asked, "Did you hear me?"

His mood had changed completely. He nodded slowly and gazed out at the road ahead, his usually brilliant eyes dark and cloudy now.

"Will you take me there sometime?"

"Maybe. Someday."

Jeffery took Lisa home early that night. Parked in her driveway, he turned solemnly to her, gazing with anguish at her lovely, classic features.

"Darling, I—" He stopped. She looked especially beautiful in the soft light of the moon that poured through the palm trees. The golden hair around her shoulders took on a radiant glow, and how he loved the way the moon's reflection caught in her eyes and swirled about like emeralds in a tiny sea! No, he couldn't tell her, he thought. He couldn't. "Forget it," he said, and climbed out of the car. He went around to open the door for her, and they walked up to the porch. Then he kissed her tenderly good night.

The summer months passed quickly into the somewhat milder days of fall, and when Jeffery finished directing Elena's picture he accepted a film offer from another studio in Southern California. Exactly when he became conscious of his love for Lisa he wasn't certain. Perhaps in the back of his mind he had always known, but he didn't like to think about those thoughts that hovered in the deep recesses of his brain. For it was there that he stored thoughts he never wanted to stir to life again. Admitting his love for Lisa would not only stir them to life, but it would break them wide open.

One night while Lisa and Jeffery were strolling along the beach, the words "I love you" poured naturally and sincerely from his lips. He had come to love her very much and he had convinced himself that it was right for them to be together. And Lisa trustingly and wonderingly told him that his love was returned. She gave him her heart freely and unconditionally; to her it was a total commitment and the beginning of a permanent one.

During this time Jeffery lived a life of which he had never dared dream. Lisa's love for him exceeded all the boundaries of love that he had ever known. She loved him with every vital part of herself. When he looked at her, he could see it. When they talked, he could hear it. When they touched, he could feel it—vibrantly. Lisa made him feel majestic, and he loved her all the more for it. They were living in a dream, and only Jeffery knew that for Lisa the dream must one day become a nightmare.

Early on a Monday morning in October Lisa was getting

ready to leave for her job at Southern Pacific Airways when
the telephone rang. She hurried from the bathroom mirror
to answer it.

"Hello, stranger."

"Brian! Where are you?"

"At home."

"It seems like you've been gone so long."

"I've been in and out, but I haven't been able to get you.
You're a busy lady these days."

"Jeffery's been taking wonderful care of me. Oh, Brian,
I'm so happy! I love Jeffery with all my heart!"

Brian knew that Lisa had been going out with Jeffery
Stewart. His sister had kept him well-informed. But he was
hardly prepared for her abrupt declaration of love for the film
director.

"Brian, are you still there?" Lisa said into the long silence
at the other end of the telephone.

"Yes, Lisa, I'm still here."

"Did you hear what I said?"

"So you and Jeffery are getting serious, huh?"

"He's everything I ever dreamed of. I just couldn't be hap-
pier. But I've missed you and all the fun times we've had.
I don't think I realized until now when you called just how
much I've missed you."

"I've missed you too, but my work keeps me *too* busy."

"You should take more time for yourself. Wouldn't it be
wonderful if you could find someone like I found Jeffery?
Then the four of us could do things together when you're
home."

"Would you like that?"

"I'd like it very much. Oh, Brian, you'll find someone someday. I know you will."

"Maybe if I had perfect blue eyes and spoke with a British
accent."

"Oh, you're teasing!"

The love for Lisa that had blossomed and grown in Brian's heart made him long to be with her after weeks of traveling. It seemed that eons of time had passed since they had even talked. And though it hurt him deeply to give up her treasured love to another man, he had no intention of forsaking her wonderful friendship. It wouldn't be so easy now to be with her, knowing that the lovely glow on her face was for someone else, but he wanted to spend time with her as they had done in the early days of their acquaintance. Perhaps, deep in his heart, he couldn't really let go of the hope that one day she would love him as much as he loved her.

But knowing Lisa as he did, if she had truly given her heart to Jeffery Stewart, she would never want it back. And yet, Brian didn't feel as if this handsome foreigner was the right man for Lisa. Of course he must love her—of that he had little doubt. And being an experienced judge of character, he realized that the Englishman was basically a fine, decent man. But something was missing—some ingredient that made the thought of that union an incomplete one. Maybe it was no more than Brian's refusal to picture Lisa with anyone but himself. Maybe it was Jeffery's lack of any Christian convictions, although that could certainly change at any time, and he prayed that it would.

Well, whatever it was that put doubt in Brian's heart, time alone would reveal the outcome of Lisa's love. If Jeffery Stewart was the man for her, then as difficult as it would be, Brian would resign himself to that. But if not...

"Do you have plans for the weekend?" Brian asked.

"We haven't made any definite plans yet."

"If you won't be seeing Jeffery, why don't you come over to my place?"

"Oh, I'm sure I'll be seeing Jeffery, and I know he'd love to come too. How is everybody?"

"They're fine."

"How's Heather doing?"

"Still feeling sorry for herself."

"I'm so sorry," she said, and another of those long, uncertain silences fell between them. "Brian?"

"Yes."

"Is anything wrong? You're happy for Jeffery and me, aren't you?"

"Everything is fine, Lisa, as long as you're happy."

"You must be tired. You work too hard. How was your trip?"

"Which one?"

She laughed into the phone. "The last one, I guess."

"We were able to make arrangements to endow an orphanage, and we set up a fund for the operation of a school for handicapped children."

"That's wonderful. You're wonderful. It's so good to hear from you."

"Well, I'd better be going so you can get to work. I just wanted to say hi. See you tomorrow."

The overnight stay at Brian's estate was delightful for Lisa. She loved being in his home again after a rather lengthy absence, and having Jeffery there made the visit complete. But more than once during the weekend she noticed a difference in Brian's attitude. He seemed the same on the outside—as attractive as ever with his shining black hair and dark brown eyes, alert and laughing behind his tinted lenses. But Lisa had come to know this man well during the course of their friendship, and she sensed that deep inside something grave was troubling her dear friend.

That evening Lisa was coming down the stairs from her room, where she had gone to freshen up for dinner, when Brian and Maude stepped into the foyer from the living room. Jeffery was behind them. Suddenly the front door opened and Heather gushed in. She had been drinking and surveyed the fortuitous gathering with a wavering eye.

"Well, well," she said, sauntering over to the Englishman. "It's been a while, handsome."

"How have you been, Heather?"

"How've I been?" she snapped. "What do you care? You've been too busy to even return my calls."

Maude excused herself to check Livy's preparations for dinner, and Heather's dark, smoldering eyes turned on Lisa. "It looks like you won the whole ballgame, Miss Goody-Two-Shoes. Obviously you're the reason Jeff has been too busy for me."

"Honey, please," Brian said, coming to her side. "Let's not have a scene."

"A scene?" shouted Heather. "We're not having a scene! I'm just talking to Jeff and Lisa. So get off my case, big brother. I've got something to say and I'm going to say it."

"You're not going to say anything to Lisa," Jeffery said smoothly. "If you have something to say, you may say it to me alone."

"Oh, I have plenty to tell you, handsome. You're so stupid you can't see through the little Sunday school teacher either. She tried to get her hooks into my brother. When she couldn't do that she went after you. How does it feel to be second choice, beautiful?"

"Oh, that's not true!" Lisa protested.

"Isn't it?" Heather cut in. "Tell me about. Tell me about how much you love Jeff?" She cast pitiful eyes on the British director. "I would've loved you too if only you'd let me." Tears came freely down her painted cheeks. "Oh, why do I lose everything?" She turned suddenly back to Lisa. "You got what you want. I hope it makes you happy. I had it one time too. Maybe someday you'll lose Jeff like I lost Eric and then you won't be so..." She stopped, her voice lost in a sob.

Brian put his arm around his sister. "Don't do this to yourself, honey."

She jerked free of his hold. "Take your hands off me! I don't need your sympathy! Save it for all those poor souls you're always trying to help. Maybe they need you, but I don't! I don't need anybody!" She whirled around and hurried up the stairs, leaving everyone in the hall staring after her, completely astonished.

It wasn't until well after dinner that Heather came down from her room dressed to go out. As she started for the front door, Jeffery intercepted her in the foyer.

"I'd like to talk to you before you leave," he said quietly.

"What about?"

"Why don't we go for a walk?"

After a moment's hesitation she came to his side and they went down the hall and out through the patio door. When they reached the beach, they strolled along for some time beneath a star-filled sky without speaking. The surf lapped gently at the edge of the shore until finally Heather's voice broke in on the calm.

"I made a fool of myself this afternoon, didn't I?" When he didn't answer she went on. "I must apologize to Lisa." When still her companion didn't speak she looked over at him. "I'm sorry, Jeff, really I am."

His vivid blue eyes cast her a soft, understanding glance. "You're going to have to get your act back together, darling. You're going to have to stop looking inward and turn out to those around you, to your family and friends, and to your son. Especially your son. He needs you the most."

Jeffery came to a stop and Heather drew up beside him. He gazed deeply and earnestly into her eyes. "Eric is the most precious possession you'll ever have. You better get up out of your self-pity and start realizing that."

Startled by his words, Heather's gaze was fastened on his face. She had never heard him speak this way before.

"To love and be loved is the greatest joy in the world," Jeffery went on. "But when the object of that love is gone, life still goes on. And your son needs you now. He lost his father and he's almost lost you. You have a lot of love to give, darling, and Eric and the rest of your family want to return that love. You have to get yourself to the place where you can see there's an empty space in your life, a void that may never be filled in quite the same way, but it can be filled. But not by me. It wasn't intended for us and you know it. Stop searching for something that doesn't exist anymore. You won't find what you're looking for in me. Your answer lies in acceptance and rebuilding. And don't reproach Lisa. She didn't take anything away from you. And hate doesn't do any good anyway. In the end it will only destroy you."

"But this is my life—I have a right to live it any way I choose."

"No, you don't. The way you live affects those around you. I think I'm just beginning to fully understand what that means. But in your case, Eric is the one most affected, and he's entitled to the best of you that you can give. Darling, it's long past the time for you to grow up and accept your responsibilities."

They resumed their walk and in a minute Heather said, "I know you're right, Jeff, but it isn't easy."

"You're only making it more difficult."

She looked up at him. "Lisa's fortunate to have a man like you. In some ways you remind me of my brother."

"That's an honor I don't deserve. Like the honor of Lisa's love."

"She adores you."

"She's young and naive. She thinks I'm something I'm not."

"I doubt that. And, Jeff, I have gotten off the track. But not with you. I could rebuild with you. I really do love you."

"Don't waste your love, darling. Lisa's already wasted hers. I only wish I was worthy." He stared out across the clear, dark ocean. His thoughts seemed to be far off.

When they returned to the house, Heather went back up to her room instead of going out as she had planned. Sunday morning she got up early and packed her clothes and those of Eric's. She had decided they would spend some time at the home of her parents in San Francisco. When she said good-bye to everyone, Jeffery smiled a secret smile at the change evident in her attitude. Perhaps he had managed one decent gesture since leaving England.

Chapter 12 ❋❋❋❋❋❋❋❋❋❋

*W*ith Jeffery hard at work on his new film, Lisa saw little of him during the weekdays, but at the close of each day they talked on the telephone, and on weekends they had quiet dinners at her cottage or went out on the town. Sometimes she cooked dinner at his apartment, and when Brian was in town they would often join him at his estate.

As the weeks passed, Lisa never ceased to marvel at the many wonders of the man she loved—like the times he brought her a gift for no reason other than to express his love for her and the happiness she gave him. One night when they were going to the theater he showed up carrying a small white box. She opened it to find a long strand of cultured pearls. On another occasion he appeared at the door with a package containing a pair of diamond earrings and matching pin. These, he had told her, were to wear with her black dress with the lace sleeves, one that he favored so much. And the first dozen roses he sent were only the beginning. He sent an array thereafter and always enclosed a tender note.

On a Saturday night in early November, Lisa dressed carefully for a formal dinner party at Sue and Mark's house. She decided to wear a floor-length yellow dress with long bouffant sleeves and a high neckline. She wore the pearls that Jeffery had given her and arranged her hair in curls at the back of her head. She fastened one of Jeffery's roses among her curls. While putting the finishing touches on her makeup, she wondered about the special occasion that Sue and Mark were celebrating. A phone call to her friends earlier that week had not yielded anything in the way of information except that they had a surprise to share.

The dashing Englishman and his beautiful lady were the last to arrive at the party. Two of the four couples Lisa did not know. The other two were close friends of Sue and Mark's whom she had met several times before.

When everyone was seated in the living room, Mark stood up and gestered to one of the couples. "With the exception of Bill and Marion—because Bill works in my office—none of you know why we're having this party."

The group nodded in agreement and he went on. "The reason we've gotten together is to celebrate my promotion."

Congratulations came from everywhere as Sue came to her feet. "Now for my part."

"You mean there's more?" someone asked.

"This is probably the most important part. We're moving to Denver, Colorado."

"*What?*" Lisa cried.

"I'm going to take over the branch office there," Mark explained with a proud smile.

"Well, I'm thrilled for you," Lisa said, "but I'm going to miss you terribly."

"No, you won't," Sue said, "you'll be completely occupied with Jeffery. And now that we've finally met him I can see why."

Everyone laughed and Lisa said, "When will you be leaving?"

"Right away," replied Mark, "as soon as we can get everything squared away here."

Following an appetizing meal and much lively conversation, Lisa and Jeffery departed. A few last-minute hugs and congratulatory remarks, and they were on their way to her cottage. During the short drive Lisa explained her close friendship with her nearest neighbors. And now that they were going away she was both happy and sad.

At Lisa's beach cottage they stood just inside the doorway. Jeffery lingered, not wanting to say good night. "I'd better go, darling," he said finally. "It's been a long day."

She slipped her arms up tenderly around his neck. "You work so hard." She kissed him playfully on the lips.

"Have to," he said, drawing her against his hard, lean strength. "It keeps up a man's self-esteem."

"You shouldn't have to worry about that. All the pictures you direct are tremendous successes."

"You're prejudiced, darling."

"By the way, when is the premiere of Elena's film?"

"The first of the year, I think"

She nestled closer to him, content in his warmth and strength. "I love you so much," she whispered.

He bent and kissed her hard on the mouth, arousing desire within him. But at last he forced himself to let her go. This was a precious gift he had been given, the gift of Lisa's innocent love, and no matter what the personal cost, he must protect it. As long as he could. And that was just it, he thought: How much longer could he pretend? The charade he carried off so well with her was plaguing him more and more.

❀   ❀   ❀

One evening shortly before Thanksgiving Day, Lisa and Jeffery had just finished dinner at her cottage and were sitting on the couch in the living room talking about the upcoming holidays. Suddenly he turned to her, anguish in his vivid gaze.

"I love you very much, darling—you know that, don't you?"

"Yes, of course I do."

"You're much more than I'm worthy of."

She stared into his handsome face. His expression was sad and troubled. "Why do you say that?"

Pangs of guilt throbbed in his heart. "Darling, you know there isn't anywhere in the world I'd rather be than here with you."

"There isn't any reason for you to be anywhere else."

He treasured her adoring gaze, wishing with all his heart that the words she had spoken were true. But they were not, and when he finally told her the truth her enchanting glow would disappear. He was responsible for her great happiness —he couldn't deny this even to himself. And within him was the power to take her happiness away. How had he ever let the situation progress so far, he pondered. He was a man highly acclaimed in his profession. He had traveled the best roads, had moved in the finest circles. He had even sat down to dine at the Queen's table. And to what end? When you took it all away, what was left? Only a man filled with shame at having betrayed one of life's most valued gifts—trust. With an aching heart Jeffery gazed tenderly at the woman who loved him. Would she ever be able to forgive him for what he had done?

"Darling, what if...if things were somehow changed between us? What if I weren't all you think I am?"

"Jeffery, I don't have any idea what you're talking about, but this much I do know—I have only to look at you and I love you."

There was blind, trusting radiance in her lovely face, and at that moment he couldn't look at the woman who loved and believed in him so much. He took her in his arms and smothered her face against his chest. He stroked her golden tresses and pressed his lips into their fragrant softness.

Lisa was puzzled by his strange attitude. "Is everything all right?" she asked in a minute.

He released her from his desperate hold. "Everything is fine," he lied. Why tell her now and spoil the holidays?

"You said something earlier about Thanksgiving."

"I've been thinking, since Brian wants everyone to spend Christmas at his place, why don't we spend Thanksgiving with my family? I haven't seen them for more than a year, and I know they'd like to meet you."

"Of course, darling. If that's what you want. But I have to be back the next day."

"We can take an early flight and spend the whole day." She examined his perfect features in silence for a moment. "You haven't said anything about going to London during the holidays."

At the end of a lengthy silence he said, "Maybe next year."

"Don't you want to see your family?"

His brilliant eyes clouded. Then he blinked hard, as if to clear away sad memories. "I'd love to see them. And London. You'd love the Christmas tree in Trafalgar Square!" he exclaimed, his blue eyes sparkling with happy memories. "It's beautiful all lit up at night, and the shops are so gaily decorated, and everyone sings carols. You'd love London at this time of year. It's so nice and crisp and everything smells so good."

"Oh, Jeffery, let's go! Let's go see your family and London! It'll be so wonderful!"

"No!"

Lisa sensed the powerful emotions that had stirred within the Englishman as he spoke of his home, and she was confused about why he was so reluctant to discuss a holiday visit. But he only shook his blonde head when she brought up the subject again, indicating that he absolutely refused to consider it any further.

"I guess Heather and Eric will be here for Christmas with Mr. and Mrs. Sommervale," she said, bringing up a new topic. "I think it's great that Heather's been behaving herself these past months. I don't know what you said in that talk you had with her, but whatever it was sure seems to have helped."

"I simply told her the truth."

"Wouldn't it be something if every problem in life could be dealt with by merely speaking the truth?"

He nodded slowly, wondering why the truth refused to fall from his lips about something as important as what he had to tell Lisa. Why didn't he just come right out and say it, he thought. But when he looked at the joy and trust in her lovely emerald eyes, he knew that he could not.

"I'm sorry Elena will have to be away on location during the Christmas holidays," Lisa said.

"When you're in production you have to keep at it."

"It'll be a great Christmas, though. Most of us together at Brian's. It'll be wonderful."

❊   ❊   ❊

It had been a wonderful holiday season, Lisa thought, looking back. It had been a joy to see her family again, even though the visit had been such a brief one, and Jeffery had completely captivated them, as she had known he would.

One of the highlights of their Thanksgiving Day visit had been the few minutes that Lisa and her mother had managed to take away from all the company. They had gone to her old room and had sat down on the bed, laughing and talking as they had done when she was a giggly teenager.

After a good 15 minutes in which Lisa had expounded on her love for Jeffery, Mrs. Palmer had said, "Whatever happened between you and Brian Sommervale? You wrote home so much about him for awhile that I thought for sure he would be the one."

"You and Sue," Lisa had laughed. "It isn't that I don't love Brian. I do. He's become the dearest friend I have."

"We've heard so much about the fine Christian things he does. Is Jeffery a Christian?"

"No, he isn't, but he's been attending church with me."

"That's a good beginning, but don't forget—except the Lord

builds the house, they labor in vain that build it." She had
smiled then. "Mr. Sommervale—now there's a house built
on the Lord."

Lisa had nodded her agreement, and then her mother had
said, "Has Jeffery asked you to marry him yet?"

"Not yet," Lisa had confided, "but I'll tell you a little secret.
I'll probably get an engagement ring for Christmas."

Christmas at Brian's home had been a joyous occasion for
Lisa. Heather seemed to have made much improvement in
her attitude about life and she had evidently quit drinking.
And a friend of Maude's had arrived from Mexico to be a
part of the festivities. ("Our Maude's in love," Livy had told
Lisa in the kitchen on Chrismas Eve. "She met her man this
summer when she and Mr. Brian were down in Mexico.")

If Brian appeared less than his usual self, Lisa was too
caught up in the celebration to take notice. On Christmas Eve
they had decorated the giant pine and then had gathered
around the piano to sing hymns and carols. They had ex-
changed gifts on Christmas morning and had feasted that day
on the array of holiday dishes that Livy had prepared.

When Jeffery took Lisa home after the long weekend and
had not proposed, she felt a gnawing sense that something
might be wrong. Jeffery had seemed strange since their
Thanksgiving visit with her family. He had been so quiet on
the flight home. And after that she had caught him watching
her with a troubled, painful kind of expression.

❋   ❋   ❋

The premiere of Elena Morrow's latest film was held at a
Hollywood theater on New Year's Eve. Elena, who was still
filming abroad, flew in for the night's festivities, and Brian
and she arrived for the gala affair with Lisa and Jeffery and
Lance Whitworth and his wife.

Outside the theater throngs of admiring fans gathered in
hopes of seeing some of the famous stars as they climbed out

of their cars and paraded down the roped-off walkway to the entrance. When Brian appeared at Elena's side, cheers went up from the crowd for one of their hometown favorites, who was as much a celebrity in his own way as any film star.

After the film presentation guests attended a party at the home of the producer. Words of praise and congratulations were plentiful that night, and Lisa proudly observed the director, awed by his tremendous ability to evoke the deepest emotions of the characters portrayed by Lance and Elena and the others in the cast. How brilliant he was, she thought, and how blessed she was that of all the women he could have, he had chosen her.

With the passing of the holidays, Jeffery found himself face to face with the task of telling Lisa what he should have told her long before. He sensed that she was starting to grow aware of the unrest in him, and he tried at various times to find the words he must say. But always he was stopped by the expression of love and innocence on her face.

At last, during the latter part of January, he made up his mind that he could not go on deceiving her any longer. One evening he took her to dinner at the inn along the beach where they had gone on their first date. After the meal they went to a party that Lance Whitworth was giving. It was Jeffery's intention to leave the party early and park at a favorite spot beside the beach for the dreaded discussion. He could not know that his plans would be hurried along by an old acquaintance at the party.

Not long after they arrived, a statuesque British woman came rushing up to them. "Jeffery! Darling! How marvelous to see you!"

"Lily." He took her hand and placed a kiss ceremoniously upon it. "I hadn't heard you were in town."

"My agent's been working on a deal for me to do a picture with Lance," she replied, looking the tall, slender Lisa up and down. "Aren't you going to introduce me, darling?"

"Lily, this is Miss Lisa Palmer."

"How do you do?" the movie star said, holding out a ring-studded hand.

"Lisa, this is Lillian Courtney." He flashed a snow-white smile. *"The* Lillian Courtney. She's a rather well-known actress in England."

"How do you do, Miss Courtney?" Lisa said in her soft drawl. "It's a pleasure to meet you."

"Oh, she's adorable," the movie star said, addressing Jeffery again. "I've been hearing good things about you. I'm so glad. You deserve it. You've had a difficult time."

She faced Lisa, showing off a brilliant smile. "I'm glad Jeffery's found happiness at last. After all, why let a thing like that come between you."

Lisa glanced up at Jeffery, giving him a perplexed stare.

"I think it's time we were leaving'" he said, not giving her a chance to protest, but taking her by the arm and starting across the floor.

"Must you leave so soon?" said Lillian Courtney. "Why, you only just arrived!"

"Excuse us, Lily," Jeffery said, "but I think we're late for an important appointment."

He propelled Lisa toward the door. After expressing his regrets to their host, he hustled her outside to his Jaguar.

Chapter 13 ✸✸✸✸✸✸✸✸✸✸

*T*hey drove along quietly until he had parked at a secluded area beside the beach. With anguish in his eyes he stared out at the blackness of night. Only a slender moon curved in the velvet sky, and the stars, partially sheltered from view by thin, moving clouds, twinkled faintly now and then. Nearby, dark waves rushed eagerly to shore, bathing the sand devotedly and rushing out again. Minutes ticked by in silence. Then at long last Jeffery faced her and spoke.

"Darling, there's something I have to tell you," he began. But when he tried to go on the words seemed to catch and choke in his throat. He swallowed slowly and tried again. "Darling, I—" He stopped, for still the words would not come. He turned away then and sat with shoulders slumped, staring out vacantly at the dark, never-ending sea. He watched the ebb and flow of the gently rolling tide, searching his soul for the strength to find the words that would destroy the woman he loved.

In a few minutes he turned back to her. She sat beside him waiting patiently, gazing at him with questioning, trusting eyes. What could he have been thinking about these past months? He had been selfish. He loved Lisa and wanted to prolong their relationship as long as possible. But it had been wrong. For her. How could he have done this to her? She loved him. She believed in him. Well, soon that would all be over. She would hate him and he couldn't blame her.

He faced her with availing eyes. "Darling, I must tell you something. Something I should have told you when we first met."

"Tell me what? Jeffery, what is all this? What was Miss Courtney talking about?"

He achingly beheld the woman who adored him, wishing with all his might that he didn't have to look upon the hurt he was about to inflict. But of all the things he was, a coward wasn't among them (not really), and so softly and slowly he said, "I love you, darling, and I never intended for you to be hurt. You believe that, don't you?"

"Yes, of course I do." She gave careful attention to the unrest on his handsome face. "Jeffery, what's wrong? I think something's been bothering you for some time. And I think it has something to do with London and why you don't want to go there. Please tell me what it is."

He drew in a long, ragged breath. "You're so sweet and precious to me, but I've betrayed your trust. You've loved me in a way that I've never been loved before, and I suppose that's why I let it go on. But I can't honor your love. I can only go on accepting it, then misuse it, and finally destroy it. Darling, I know you've been thinking we'll be married soon, but I can't marry you. I'm already married. I have a wife back home in London."

Jeffery's words stung in her ears and tore at her heart, and for a moment she was unwilling to let her mind accept what he had said. She had never thought anyone could be as wonderful as he was, and not in her wildest dreams had she ever imagined a relationship as perfect as theirs had been. When the full impact of what he said hit her, she wanted to cry, to run and hide, to get out of the car and go and keep on going till she could go no more. Instead, she sat calmly at his side listening to the words that rocked her world apart and left her life in a shambles beneath her feet.

"I know I should have been honest with you from the beginning, but it didn't seem important at first. It seems like I'm not married. But I know I am. Most people who know about us think we were divorced years ago. Lily is a dear friend. And she knows the truth. But I've been separated for a long time. And I've asked for a divorce many times. My attorney has the papers drawn up agreeing to whatever she wants, but she's contesting. We don't have the flexible divorce laws that you have in the States. In England both parties have to agree. I've offered her everything I have, but she won't let me go."

"*Why?*" It was a desperate cry.

"I don't know. Power, I suppose. She knows she can hold me and she's doing it. Maybe she thinks I'll come back to her someday."

"Will you?" she questioned bitterly.

"No. I never loved her really. When we met I was a struggling young actor. I thought she was special. After we were married I soon found out how wrong I was. I don't like to speak out against any woman, but the truth is she's a cunning, selfish, egotistical brat." He stopped sharply and heaved a deep, painful sigh. "Darling, that's not all."

Not all, thought Lisa. Oh, dear God, in the name of all that was right and good, what more could there be? She tried to brace herself for whatever he would say next, but nothing prepared her for his coming words.

"Darling...darling, I have a son too." He rushed on before she could respond, as though he had to get it all said while he still could. "When our son was born, I tried to work things out. After awhile I saw how impossible it was, so I left. I went back once, only for the boy's sake—I wanted it to work for my son."

"*Your son!*" Lisa glared at him, forcing back the soul-burning tears. "Oh, Jeffery, why didn't you tell me? Didn't you think I had a right to know?"

"Of course. And I tried, but it was so hard. Before meeting you, I'd come to the point where I would never even think about her anymore. I don't feel married anymore, so at first our relationship seemed proper and natural."

"And what about your son—don't you ever think about him anymore?" she charged coldly. "Don't you feel like a father anymore?"

"Of course I do." A painful expression crossed his magnificent face. "I think about my son almost all the time, but what good does it do me? His mother won't even let me see him."

This stirred compassion in Lisa's heart, but she was much too hurt just then to share in his pain. All that Jeffery had told her had come as quite a shock. And it hurt deeply, more deeply than anything she had ever experienced. She was too stunned to even think clearly.

"Please, let's not talk about it anymore tonight. Just take me home."

At Lisa's cottage Jeffery parked in the paved drive. "I'll call you tomorrow."

"No. We'd better not see each other anymore."

"Darling—"

"Please, Jeffery, don't make it any harder than it is." She sadly regarded the man she had come to love so much, and tears scalded her emerald eyes. "I'm sorry," she managed, and got out of the car and ran inside.

In the days and nights that followed, Lisa vented the hurt and anger that raged within her. Tears ran unchecked down her sunny cheeks as she cried out the shock and indignity of Jeffery's words. She had loved him with all her heart, had placed in him her every trust. But he had betrayed her. Knowing he was married to another, he had let her naturally assume they would wed. How he could do that to her was a question she asked herself a thousand tormenting times.

When the initial impact wore off, Lisa told herself that her love for Jeffery Stewart was a thing of the past. She had made a mistake, she had fallen in love with a married man, but she hadn't known. Oh, she hadn't known! And now it was over and done. She asked God to forgive her mistake and vowed to start her life anew.

But time passed slowly, and she missed Jeffery and the life they had shared. She wondered what he was doing and if he missed her. Often she longed to just pick up the phone and call him. If only she could hear the sound of his voice one more time. If only she could look into his beautiful eyes, smile into his handsome face. If only...

But a clean break was the best. What good would it do to talk to him? What good could come from seeing him? Theirs was a love that could not be. And with God's help she would survive the hurt. *This too shall pass,* He told her in her prayers. And while she knew it was true and felt His comforting presence, still it was hard to endure.

One evening a few days after her parting with Jeffery the telephone rang while Lisa was in the kitchen trying to exhaust herself in a major cleanup job. It was Brian.

"It's nice of you to call," she said, trying to sound natural. She had told no one of her breakup with Jeffery. Since Sue and Mark had moved to Denver, she had not been as close to anyone else. Except Brian.

And the sensitive Brian, whose way of life was other people's problems, was quick to perceive that something was wrong with Lisa. "Are you all right?"

"Yes, I-I'm fine." She tried to steady the quivering of her words, but the philanthropist could not be fooled.

"What is it, Lisa?"

Her voice caught in her throat and she couldn't go on.

"Lisa! Lisa, answer me!"

She couldn't. She was crying.

"I'm coming over," Brian said. "I'll be there in 20 minutes."

Brian Sommervale had seen it all in his lifetime and

experience—everything from homeless children wandering aimlessly in filthy streets to drug addicts climbing the walls during withdrawal. He had shared hundreds of tormenting experiences with all kinds of people, but nothing had touched him so deeply as the look on Lisa's face when she opened the door. Her sweet glow was gone. The fresh joy that had surrounded her was not there anymore. The laughter and fun that had been a way of life had vanished. She no longer seemed young and carefree and tender. And what was it about the look in her eyes that reminded him so much of Heather?

He put his arm around her and led her over to the couch. They sat down and she laid her head against his shoulder, her tears suddenly flooding his shirt as she tried once again to cry away the hurt. He held her lovingly and soothingly, but it was a little while before Lisa could coherently speak to him.

When at last it seemed no more tears could come, she regained some of her composure and began telling Brian the heartbreaking news that Jeffery had finally shared with her.

"He has a wife and child. Two people in this world bear his name. Sometimes I still can't believe it. We were so happy. Our love was so beautiful. I thought he was going to propose during the holidays. Why does it have to be this way, Brian, tell me why?"

"I can't tell you why, Lisa. I've seen things in this world that would be hard for most people to even admit to, let alone look upon. I used to think surely there can't be a reason, but I've learned not to question anymore. We'll understand one day."

"But how could he do this to me, how could he?"

"Maybe he was a little too much a man of the world for you. But you're growing up fast."

"Brian, did you know Jeffery was married?"

His dark eyes widened behind the tinted lenses he wore.
"I didn't have any idea."

"Did Heather know?"

"I'm sure she didn't. You know my sister—she wouldn't
have been able to keep *that* a secret."

"No, she would have been in her glory if she could have
dropped that piece of information in my lap." She gazed at
him without speaking for a minute. "I don't see how two
people as closely related as you and Heather can be so
totally different."

"I guess I'm the one who's different."

"If you had known about Jeffery, would you have told me?"

Brian laughed at her typically feminine line of reasoning.
"Sure I'd have told you. Do you think I'd have let you go
through all this if I'd known?"

"No, of course you wouldn't. I'm sorry for even asking."

"What he told you wasn't exactly everyday news. I'm sure
he realizes what you're going through."

"It may be more everyday news than you think. When
I look back I can see how naive I was. I should have known
a man like him couldn't have escaped marriage all his life."

"I wouldn't say that. I've managed to keep my freedom."

"Yes, but you're different."

He flashed his slightly crooked smile. "We've covered
that."

"You know what I mean."

"Yes, I know. You think I'm some lunatic they let out
because of my sunny smile and winning ways."

"Oh, you nut!"

"See, what did I tell you?" Brian laughed his all-consuming
laugh and Lisa laughed with him.

"That's the best sound I've heard all day," she said.

"What?"

"Your laughter. It's so real and so beautiful. It makes me
feel good all over." She gazed fondly at him. How she had

been missing her dear friend and his kind, wholesome companionship! But she had everything she needed in Jeffery—she thought.

Brian was sympathetic as Lisa and he sat and talked. And he was careful not to reproach Jeffery Stewart in any way, not then or ever. He was much too intelligent to render judgment on any person or circumstances, realizing that he could never truly understand what another person would do in a given situation unless he had lived that person's life. Anyway, he felt sure Jeffery had meant well. And as for Lisa? He could only hurt for her unhappiness and find himself wishing that the famous film director had not left England in the first place and that he had had more time to win her love for his own.

When Brian finally got up to leave, Lisa went with him to the door. "Thank you for coming over," she said, and they stood gazing at each other.

"You don't have to thank me." He moved closer, brushing an imaginary tear from her cheek. "I'll come anytime."

His dark gaze held hers compellingly, and she was puzzled by what she saw in his eyes. Why at the moment did his expression remind her so much of Jeffery?

"You're the best friend anyone could have," she said, and suddenly felt his hand take hers.

"You'd better get some sleep." He gave her his beautiful smile. "If you need me, just reach out and I'll be there."

Chapter 14 ✳✳✳✳✳✳✳✳✳✳

*L*isa was at the table in her kitchen, going over the Bible lesson for her Wednesday night class when the doorbell rang. It was Friday evening, two weeks after her parting with Jeffery, and if she had had strong moments when she didn't even think of him, there were more times when she did—times when he occupied her every thought, times when she asked herself, what if? What if he hadn't been married? What if he could get his wife to give him a divorce? What if they just tried to go on as they were? How easy it would be to just accept the world's standard, to take Jeffery on any terms, even at the cost of her faith and values.

But she knew she could not. Never could she have imagined having to make such a decision in her young life. But Jesus said that a Christian is *in* the world but not *of* the world. He said: When you follow me you deny yourself; when you love me you keep my commandments, and you must give up even your loved ones if they would keep you from me.

In her heart Lisa knew that Jesus would never ask anything of her that He would not give her the strength to do. It would take time to recover from her loss, her pain. It would take time to get over her love. But He would not let her down. Of that she was certain.

When Lisa opened the front door a gasp of disbelief caught in her throat.

"May I come in?"

A stab of pain pierced her heart when she looked up into his splendid face, and in her moment of hesitation Jeffery said, "I won't stay long. I'm on my way to the airport. But I couldn't leave without talking to you."

She moved aside for him to enter the room, and when she had closed the door and motioned him to sit down he strode to the couch. She took a seat in the big chair by the door.

"You're leaving? Going back to London?"

"Yes. But I couldn't go, not without saying good-bye and telling you one more time how sorry I am for what I did."

She was seeing him again, thought Lisa, seeing his beautiful face, hearing his wonderful voice. Oh, it would be so easy to give in, just to be with him, even for a little while longer. But she couldn't. She mustn't. He belonged to another, even though that wasn't what he wanted. But he could never really belong to her. And as painful as their parting was, she truly did not want him any other way.

Please, God, she prayed silently, *You know I'm crumbling apart inside. Please give me the courage to let go completely.*

In a minute she said, "Jeffery, I want you to know that I don't blame you. In a way we were victims of circumstances beyond our control."

"I don't deserve your forgiveness. You put your trust in me and I failed you. That's partly why I wanted to see you before I left. I wanted you to know that I understand that we can't see each other anymore. I know our relationship has to end—for you. But I'm just so sorry I failed you."

"But you didn't fail me. Telling me about your wife and son must have been the hardest thing you've ever had to do."

"You're giving me credit I don't deserve. I couldn't offer you what you deserve. I had to tell you sooner or later. But the hardest thing was asking my wife for a divorce—again. I talked to her this week. I was hoping...but I should've known. When I left she swore she would never stop getting even."

"Is that why she won't let you see your little boy?"

He nodded.

"That seems such a cruel thing for anyone to do, especially to him."

"But maybe it isn't any more than I deserve."

"No. Whatever happened between you and your wife, she has no right to keep you from seeing you son."

"I'm going to see him when I get back. I've made up my mind to that."

She smiled at him. "I'm glad. Jeffery, would you do something else when you get back to London? You've been going to church with me. Would you—"

"Lisa, I don't—"

"All right," she broke in, unable to hear him reject the only thing that was holding her world together. "I won't ask you anything more. It's just that I wish you could have what Brian and I have."

What Brian and you have, thought Jeffery. Well, he didn't know anything about that, but he remembered what Heather had said once about Lisa being in love with her brother. She wasn't, of course, but maybe all these two needed was another chance to have each other.

❋　❋　❋

The next morning Lisa was rudely summoned from a deep sleep by a persistent chiming of the doorbell. She dragged her sluggish body from the couch and stumbled across the room. At the turn of the doorknob a cheerful hunk of humanity burst inside. He was dressed in white tailored slacks and yellow silk shirt that heightened the bronze of his skin.

Brian appraised her disheveled appearance. "You really had a good one, didn't you?"

She walked down the hall to the bathroom and peered

into the mirror over the vanity. Her green eyes were red and puffy, her hair was a mass of golden tangles, and what she could see of her blue dress looked hopelessly wrinkled. After Jeffery had gone Lisa had cried herself to sleep on the couch. She hadn't even bothered to go to bed.

"This dress is supposed to be permanent press," she said, gazing into the mirror at the lively image that came up behind her.

"It looks like permanent wrinkles to me." With a cheerful, carefree bounce, he started down the hall. "Take a shower and get cleaned up while I cook breakfast."

She followed him into the kitchen. "I didn't know you could cook."

"I've managed to keep a few secrets." He faced her. "Now scoot. I can't do it looking at you. You're a mess."

She smiled her wide, even smile and went back along the hall to the bath, leaving Brian whistling merrily to himself and digging randomly in a cupboard for pots and pans. When she returned to the kitchen wearing a pantsuit in a pale shade of pink and sat down at the table, he was pouring two cups of coffee.

His dark eyes studied her thoughtfully. "You look absolutely gorgeous."

"You say the sweetest things," she said as she stared at the huge pile of scrambled eggs, crisp bacon, and buttered toast that Brian had prepared. "Did you really cook all this?"

"Not really," he said with such nonchalance that she almost believed him. "I carry this little genie around in a bottle with me wherever I—"

Lisa's slender body shook with laughter. "Oh, Brian, you're ridiculous."

"Well, I should hope so. After all these years of practice."

She laughed again and said, "But I can't eat all this."

He took the chair across from her. "I hope not. I'm planning on eating some of it myself." After he offered a prayer of thanks, Brian reached for a piece of toast. "How'd it go last night?"

She looked dumbfounded. "How did you know?"

"Jeffery called and told me he was flying back to London and that he wanted to say good-bye to you."

"And wise man that you are, you knew how well I'd handle it."

"I don't call that wise. It's the hardest thing in the world to say good-bye to someone you love."

She gazed across the table at him for a moment. "Well, thank you for coming over. I don't know what I'd do without you."

His mouth widened, one corner lifting higher than the other. "I was in that same boat one time."

They laughed at his humorous play on words, and then he went on. "You don't have to thank me. I'd do anything for you. I'd give you the whole world and everything in it, only..."

"Only what?"

"Only the one thing you want, I can't get for you."

"Maybe you can't give me what I want, but you can give me what I need—your friendship."

"You've always had that."

"But I don't want to be a bother to you now. You're so busy."

"I'm not too busy for you."

"You wouldn't tell me if you were."

"I'm not, that's all. Not ever again."

She gazed sweetly at him. "I don't know how you do it all, taking on everyone's problems. You never complain. Don't you ever wish you didn't have to go somewhere and help someone?"

"I don't have to go—I go because I want to."

"I know, but don't you ever wake up in the morning not wanting to look at another hungry child?"

"No, Lisa. I'll go as long as there's breath in my body,

because until we've helped fill their empty stomachs we can't begin to approach their souls. And their souls are what's so important."

"You make me ashamed. You're so unselfish."

"Maybe it's a lot more selfish than it sounds. Everything I do gives me a deep sense of satisfaction and well-being."

"And what's wrong with that? I know the credit belongs to God, but you let Him use you. It's your choice."

"I know." He laughed his wonderful, rich laugh and she gazed at the sweet magnetism in his face. "I guess I'm just a terrific guy."

She laughed with him. "You're teasing me."

"It's good to hear you laugh—again."

"Well, here's a laugh for you: I certainly haven't lived a very unselfish life. I was so sure Jeffery was what I needed. I've been a weak Christian, letting him mean more to me than he should have."

Gazing at Brian, she pondered what great spiritual strength was harnessed in his humanity, and wished she had his self-discipline. And though she knew his power came from God, she wondered if sometimes he didn't need someone special to share his life. She could only think of the long days and nights without Jeffery in her life, and she knew how difficult it was.

"Brian, I know you said you aren't looking for a wife, but don't you sometimes wish for a companion, someone to help carry the load?"

His brown eyes glanced briefly at her behind his wire-framed glassed. "Maybe. Sometimes."

"Do you think you'll ever get married?"

"I don't know."

"Haven't you ever been in love?"

"There was this one girl in college, but I guess I've really only been in love once."

"What happened?"

He kept his eyes leveled on her face, "I fell in love with her, but she fell in love with someone else."

"Oh, I'm sorry."

"I'm sorry too."

"I don't know how you'd ever have time to fall in love, as busy as you are."

"Sometimes it just happens even when you're not conscious of taking any time to work at it."

"I guess without Maude you wouldn't have what little time you do have."

"I couldn't manage without Maude." He stared deeply into her eyes. "Or someone like her. I have to have some kind of secretary. Maude is very dedicated to the work we do. I appreciate that." He paused reflectively. "You know, sometimes I've wished I was just an ordinary man," he admittted, "just like every other guy, with a home and family and bills to pay. But God didn't choose that kind of life for me. And no matter what I wanted, I'd be miseraable if I weren't doing what He wanted."

"Yes, I know—now."

"What are your plans for the day?" Brian said in a minute.

"I don't really have any."

"I have a lunch date in Oakland with a friend who works in the public defender's office. Would you like to go with me?"

"I wouldn't want to intrude on a date."

"It's with a man."

"Oh," she said, grinning playfully. "Is that another one of your well-kept secrets?"

He gave her a crooked, teasing little smile. "Now you know the real reason I've never married."

"Oh, sure," she laughed.

"Would you like to go with me?"

"Yes, if you want me to."

"He wants me to help him with a case he's working on—a

young man accused of armed robbery. I don't know what
he thinks I can do, but he called early this morning and said
it was urgent that we talk. Whatever he wants, I'm sure we'll
be back by tonight.''

Lisa's expression was serious and thoughtful as she gazed
across the breakfast table into Brian's handsome bronze
features. He looked tired this morning. Yet here he was doing his best to cheer her, and even while doing that he was
about to go off to help someone else. How unfair it seemed
all of a sudden! One person shouldn't have to bear so much
responsibility. But perhaps that was the price he had to pay
for being so compassionate, so generous, so understanding.
Everything in life, it appeared, had its price—even goodness.

Chapter 15 ✸✸✸✸✸✸✸✸✸✸

*L*ate that afternoon as they were leaving the courthouse in Oakland, Brian addressed Lisa. "You want to fly back to Brenthall for dinner or hang around here and eat?

"Whatever you want to do is okay with me."

"Why don't we go now? You can fly us back."

"Oh, Brian, I don't know. It's been awhile since I've been up."

"I'll handle the takeoff, since you aren't qualified in my plane. You can take over when we get up."

He hailed a cab that took them to the airport, and after checking out the jet they left for home. Lisa was thrilled to be at the controls of a plane again. It felt good to be in the air, soaring above the world, free in the wind, and she handled the aircraft as if she had never been away from flying.

When they landed at Brenthall, Lisa was bursting with excitement. "I didn't know how much I missed flying."

"It gets to you that way."

"You know, Brian, I'm going to have some time on my hands now. I think I'll go to school and get my commercial license. Maybe I could get into flying in a serious way."

"You'd really like that, wouldn't you? Flying a lot?" When she nodded eagerly, he said, "Let me help you get started."

They were leaving the hangar where he kept his Lear jet.

She drew up sharply beside him. "No, Brian. Don't even think about it. I won't let you."

"But do you make enough to meet all your expenses and pay for your training too?"

"Vic and Jerry pay me very well. I can manage just fine."

They arrived at his sports car and his dark gaze met hers. "Let me pay for your training. I want to do this for you."

"You've given me everything else, but I couldn't take money from you."

He placed his hands on her shoulders. "Lisa, don't you know that money is worthless if it isn't used to help people? It's just old cut-up pieces of paper if it lies around in a bank somewhere. Money's meant to be spread around. The more happiness it helps create, the more it's worth."

"Please, Brian, I can't accept it from you. Everybody takes everything from you. I only want to give."

He resisted a sudden, strong urge to take Lisa in his arms. He dropped his hands from her shoulders. "I can help strangers, but not my friends?"

"No, but..."

"That's not a good enough answer."

"Come on, let's get some dinner. I'm famished."

"Let me make you a loan. You can pay me back later."

She looked like she was going to laugh. "You know you'd never let me."

"You haven't heard the last of this."

I know, she thought with a smile. Arguing with Brian Sommervale was like trying to launch a spaceship from your backyard: You might get off the pad, but you didn't stay in orbit very long.

At a favorite restaurant in Brenthall, Lisa and Brian talked casually while they ate, but there was no more mention of money. At least not then.

"How long have you been a pilot?" Lisa asked.

"I've been flying for several years now. When I first started traveling a lot, I flew a commercial line. Then I bought a small jet similar to the one I have now. I hired a pilot to fly it, but I was always in the cockpit with him. All those gauges and dials and switches really fascinated me. I always wanted to do the flying myself. So I studied and trained, and it took awhile, but finally I got all my credentials and I've been flying ever since."

"How did you ever find the time?"

"I just took the time. I knew it would help my work in the long run. I enjoy doing the flying, and it's simpler this way."

"That means a lot to you, doesn't it?"

"Keeping it simple? Yes. I could staff a large organization, and I've thought about it, because we could meet more needs and meet them quicker. But no matter how hard I tried I couldn't keep up with them all. And that's one of the things I like best about my work—the personal involvement in each situation. And it's necessary to me. You'd be surprised how many phonies I encounter."

"How can you know when you encounter someone like that?"

He shrugged his broad shoulders. "I don't know. But I can spot a phony a mile away. I guess it's because I've been exposed to so many different kinds of people. And then we investigate each cause thoroughly and act on God's guidance. Most people aren't aware that a very small percentage of what they donate to charity, even the ones that are well-known and trustworthy, actually goes to the need it was collected for. And there are so many rackets going on—people who claim to have needs but really don't, and people who use needy causes for their own gain. And the critics. You wouldn't believe it."

"Critics? You mean people actually criticize what you do? I've never heard anything but praise about you."

"The world is full of self-appointed critics. But I don't let them bother me."

"What could anyone find to criticize in your life?"

"Are you kidding? Lisa, I've never worked a day in my life to earn a dollar. Do you have any idea of the kind of jealousy that causes? And there are a lot of people who think I shouldn't spend my money outside the United States."

"But—"

"Let's just drop it," he said. "It's not important. I don't have to answer to any man—only God." After a pause, he said, "Lisa, are you happy at Southern Pacific? You're still content to stay there indefinitely?"

"Of course. Why?"

"I need you. That is...I could use you."

"You have a wonderful secretary."

"No, I'm not talking about that part of it. You could help me with the flying. We'd make a great team."

"Wouldn't that make your organization too big if you took on a co-pilot?" She delivered this with a playful, mocking smile.

"I can handle it."

But Lisa shook her blonde head emphatically. "No. But thank you for offering. I love you for caring so much. And I can afford to pay for the rest of my training. It's no problem, really."

"I never said it was a problem. Sometimes I just like to do things for people I care about."

She gazed affectionately into his bronze face. "May I tell you something?"

Brian ran his tongue along the edges of his perfect white teeth. "I'd say no, but you'll tell me anyway. So go ahead— just don't pile it too high, though."

She stared at him for a full minute, then slowly a smile crept over her sunny features. "You're crazy," she said.

He laughed his beautifully, soul-deep laugh. "I understand an opinion of that sort has been circulating for some time."

"You're the most wonderful and crazy person I know. And

I want you to know how much I appreciate you taking time to be with me right now."

"I'm going to stay in town awhile longer. So if you need me for anything, just call me."

"How can I ever thank you for...for being you?"

He leaned over and placed of soft, sweet kiss on her cheek. "That's all the thanks I need for anything. And I want you to know how sorry I am about what happened. I wish you could have had what you wanted." Behind the tinted lenses he wore, his dark gaze held hers compellingly. "But in time you'll...you'll be all right."

"I know." She smiled her wide, even smile. "If you don't have any plans for next weekend, I'd like to come over."

Saturday morning Lisa drove to Brian's estate as she had done countless times in days gone by, and following an exuberant greeting by the household staff she went upstairs to the pink-and-white room where she always stayed. There she took a mental journey back in time to the first weekend she had visited, when they had held the press conference. But when her thoughts stirred to the evening when she had painstakingly dressed in hopes of attracting Jeffery's attention, her gaiety vanished suddenly. She blinked away hot, painful tears and could feel herself dancing across the patio in his strong arms. The softness of his first kiss on the beach came as fresh to her mind as yesterday, and she knew that nothing could possibly hurt as much as remembering those wonderful days of their love and companionship. But remembering was not what she needed to do, so she forced away her tender reveries and crossed the room to the French doors. She flung them open, as though a gust of warm sea air would clear the room of the sweet, silent intrusions that floated about her.

On the balcony she surveyed the striking view of the endless blue sea and drew in a long, deep breath of salty air. Memory was about to overtake her once again when she saw

Brian in the distance. He was coming toward the house and she watched as he ambled along, gently kicking the sand beneath his bare feet. When he drew near he caught sight of her and waved a hand, beckoning her to join him. She smiled her agreement and waved back, thinking what a truly wonderful man he was. As she left the room to meet him a strange new thrill surged through her. But she paused over it only momentarily, wondering at the pounding of her heart when she saw him just now. Why should her heart hammer this way at the sight of her friend? Perhaps it was her mood and the reflections of Jeffery. Maybe seeing Brian on the beach reminded her of the times spent there with the Englishman.

But it was too soon since her parting with Jeffery, and she was too bound by memories to discern the possibility before her.

Later, when Lisa and Brian returned from their long walk, which turned into a long ride when they saddled two stallions from the stable, she went up to her room to dress for dinner. After Brian showered and changed, he came down to find his sister on the couch in the living room. She had been gone all day and had come back in a slightly intoxicated condition.

"Where's Lisa?" she asked, looking up as he entered the living room. "Maude said she's here for the weekend."

"She's upstairs changing for dinner."

"I don't know how she did it," Heather said. "I don't know how she let Jeff go. If he had loved me, I'd never have given him up."

He took a place beside her. "Maybe it has something to do with innate honesty and a God-fearing conviction of what's right and wrong."

Heather's dark eyes glinted mischievously. "Is that what Lisa's been doing this past year? Living up to her God-fearing convictions?"

"She didn't know."

"Would it have made any difference?"

"It seemed to. As soon as he told her."

"He's a fool," she said, and watched her brother for a moment behind thick, drooping lashes. "Haven't you been home a long time?"

"I can't go anywhere right now."

"You mean you *won't*. You think you have to stay here and play the patron saint to Lisa. But it won't do you any good. She'll never come to you. She's too much in love with Jeff. She won't forget him for a long time."

Brian was taken aback by her remark. He hadn't known his sister had realized how he felt about Lisa. "I'll wait."

After the evening meal Brian came back to the living room and sat down at the piano. Lisa found him there later, softly playing a favored hymn. She stopped in the doorway and listened to the pure, sweet sound. Sensing her presence perhaps, he looked up. Then he smiled.

"Come here, Lisa."

"I was just enjoying. I don't want to disturb you."

"You aren't disturbing me." He stopped playing and patted the bench beside him. "Come and sit down."

She crossed the room to the piano and took a place next to him. "Can you play with me sitting here?"

For an answer he played two more favorite hymns.

"You really are rich, aren't you?" she said when he stopped again. "I mean you put your fingers on the keys and the most beautiful sound comes out. That's great wealth."

He smiled his smile that could light up the world. "Thank you."

"Play something else."

"What would you like to hear?"

"Anything. Play whatever you want."

Brian placed his gifted fingers on the ivory keys once more and a sudden, peaceful melody filled the room. It was some time later, when Peter served coffee, that they left the piano and sat talking quietly on the couch.

"Did Heather go up to bed?" Lisa asked. "She was really a mess at dinner."

A painful look crossed Brian's handsome face. "Yes."

"I feel so sorry for her. What happened? She was doing so well at Christmas."

"I don't know. I guess she just couldn't stop drinking. And now it seems like she's trying to drink herself into oblivion."

"What will it take to stop her, I wonder?"

Chapter 16 **********

*I*t was the following afternoon when Brian got the phone call. Lisa was so excited she could scarcely talk at first.

"Oh, Brian, you'll never guess! Vic and Jerry have decided to buy another plane! They've started interviewing pilots, but when I told them I was going to work on my commercial license they said I might be able to do some flying for them!"

"That's great, Lisa!"

"I think after I get my license and start flying, I'll use the extra money I earn to finish college. I can take night classes."

Lisa plunged wholeheartedly into the completion of her flight training. She enrolled in the courses needed to get her commercial license, which differed from her previous learning in that it involved more intense and advanced training, more flying hours, more advanced maneuvers and closer tolerances, and at least three cross-country flights. At the same time she began the mandatory 40 hours of training necessary for her instrument rating, which involved flying by instruments alone, without any visual aids.

Her days were spent as usual, behind the desk at the office of Southern Pacific Airways, and her nights were taken up by poring over books and spending many hours in the flight simulator. And if occasionally her longing for Jeffery still became overpowering, the passing of each busy day seemed to make the tears come less often. It would take time to heal the hurt and adjust to the loss of what could not be, but she was surviving as God had assured her she would.

Brian continued to remain at his estate in Brenthall, attending to the never-ending requests for money to aid one project or another. He found himself inspired by an outstanding new school being formed to educate retarded children, and another designed to instruct hearing-impaired children. He made frequent trips to the schools to view their progress.

He used some of this time to help children whose parents were on drugs and children themselves who fell victim to this horrible villain. And he gave special attention to physically and emotionally abused children, volunteering his time to work personally with these most desolate of God's children.

When Lisa had some free time on weekends, Brian took her with him to visit nursing homes, children's hospitals, and orphanages. And there were trips taking underprivileged and disabled children to Disneyland, to the zoo in San Diego, and to other places of fun and interest. On these visits and outings Lisa watched and marveled at her compassionate friend, for it seemed there was nothing he could not or would not do for other people. No kind of human need appeared strange to him.

"How did you happen to get started in the business of helping others?" Lisa asked Brian one Saturday morning as they were driving to a nearby orphanage.

"How can you live in the world and not know people are hurting? And there's a danger in being rich, I think. The danger lies in the temptation to do other than what pleases God. Because I have been given so much, I know that God requires much from me. The Bible plainly says so." Brian grew strangely quiet for a moment. And then: "I've watched helpless little kids die because they didn't get enough to eat. I've held their bloated little bodies in my arms. I've—" He stopped. "Their bony little hands reach out, their big sorrowful eyes plead." He shook his dark, shiny head. "How can I turn away? It's the kids who get to me the most. I just want to help them while they're still children, while they're young—before they grow up and learn how to hate."

"You've seen so much hurting."

"Sometimes I don't think I can let any more hurt touch me." He shrugged his broad shoulders. "Maybe I'm beginning to lose my grip. But how do I stop? Where do I stop? I don't want to."

"What a task you've taken on!"

He ran one hand absently through his beautiful black hair. "I decided a long time ago that every human being in the world is born with three rights—the right to have enough to eat, the right to be free and develop his potential, and the right to have a chance to know God. I'll die before all that's accomplished. We all will. But till then..."

"Brian, why is it that when we talk about your work, I feel like I don't do much for the Lord?"

"If you feel that way, maybe there's something else you need to be doing. But I'm not qualified to make a judgment like that. I can only live the kind of life that's right for me. It's a full-time job taking care of Brian Sommervale's business. I don't have time to examine what anyone else is doing or not doing." He smiled over at her. "But anytime you want to join me full-time, the offer's still open."

Lisa gazed at the man behind the wire-rimmed glasses, and having known him for some time now she found herself still in his awe. And that awe was heightened as she watched his instant rapport with the children of the orphanage. It saddened her heart as they visited with each child, some returning smiles but others only looking forlornly. Yet she was filled with joy at seeing Brian's natural love for humanity, especially children, come to life before her eyes. She watched his smiling face and listened to the tenderness in his rich voice as he played and talked with the children nobody wanted.

"What a bright light you are!" she told him near the end of their visit.

"I'm not even a flickering candle," he said.

"Didn't someone once say that it's better to light one candle than to stand and curse the darkness?"

"I feel the only hope for improving the world is in leaving a legacy of love to the children. If just one child can see the love of Jesus through me then I've accomplished God's purpose in giving me life. You asked me how I got started helping people. You know how it really began? It began when I was born, or even before that. I was richly blessed with what really matters in life. I was born into a home filled with love. My parents disciplined me—they were firm and steady—but they also lavished me with love. A person learns to give love by getting it. Loving comes easy for me because I've been loved all my life. I've always known I mattered to someone. And that's what it's all about. Everyone needs to know he makes a difference in someone's life."

"Brian, I don't think it's *what you do* that matters as much as *why you do it.* I'm just beginning to realize that it doesn't matter what you do—whether you have a little to give or a lot—it's just giving *yourself* that counts."

❋   ❋   ❋

One night in early summer Lisa had gone to bed and dreamed about Jeffery. In her dream he had returned and stood waiting for her on the porch. Awakened about three o'clock, she jumped up and ran to the front door, such was the reality of her fantasy. She opened it and peered out into the night, but found only darkness and stillness as black and hushed as death itself. She closed the door and went back to the bedroom. But she only stood in the middle of the floor staring at the bed. She knew she couldn't sleep. In the dream the yearning for Jeffery had become almost unbearable. And she had been doing so well!

She wandered out to the kitchen and made a cup of hot cocoa. But she couldn't drink it. She came back to the bedroom and paced back and forth across the carpet, wishing fervently that she was not alone.

The strident ringing of the telephone took her by surprise. Phone calls in the middle of the night always scared her. Had something happened to someone in her family?

"Hello?" she said cautiously into the receiver.

"It's Brian, Lisa. I'm sorry to wake you."

"You didn't. I was up."

"You know, it's strange, but I woke up a few minutes ago and had the strongest urge to call you."

"I'm glad you did."

"What are you doing up at this hour?"

"Oh...I couldn't sleep."

"Is anything wrong?"

"No, I'm all right."

"Would you like some company?'

She smiled at the telephone. Did Brian sense she didn't want to be alone? Did he sense that it had something to do with Jeffery? He was unbelievable. And wonderful.

"Brian, I don't want you coming out in the middle of the night."

"Since when do you tell me what to do, young lady?"

She laughed. He was hopeless. And a prince.

"I'll be there in 20 minutes."

While she waited for Brian, Lisa put on a robe and walked around her cottage thinking about her dream and remembering Jeffery's splendid love. She recalled the excitement of his kisses, the thrill of his gentle touch, the tender glances from his vivid eyes. By the time Brian arrived she was feeling miserable again. He sat beside her listening attentively while she told him about her dream.

"I don't think I'm going to make it after all," she finished lamely. "It's wretched without him. I could see Jeffery so clearly. I could hear him talking. Oh, Brian, I miss him so much!"

"I know you do, Lisa. I know how much it hurts. I just wish I could hurt for you."

The tenderness in his voice touched her. And when she looked over at him, there was no mistaking the expression on his handsome face.

"If only I could make you forget him," he said, his voice husky now with emotion and his face a picture of love and tenderness.

Suddenly it all fell in place for her: Brian's lack of enthusiasm when she first told him about her love for Jeffery; the feeling she had had that something had been troubling her friend; even his attentiveness now and the way he looked at her sometimes.

"I fell in love with her, but she fell in love with someone else."

It had been there all the time: the whisper of his love. But she hadn't heard it.

Alarmed, Lisa rose and crossed the room. She stood with her back to him. Brian came to her and placed his hands on her shoulders. In a minute he turned her around and took her hands in his. She stood before him with eyes downcast, her long hair brushing gently across her shoulders. He lifted one hand and tilted her chin upward, forcing her to look at him. The new anguish he saw in her expression told him that he had given himself away, that his secret love was a secret no more.

"I didn't intend for you to find out like this," he said at last.

"Oh, Brian..." That was all she could say.

In spite of her protest she presented a lovely picture with her golden hair, her sparkling eyes and flowing robe. He was caught up in his long unrequited love for her. He wanted to take her in his arms and whisper tender endearments to soothe her. He longed to kiss her lips and wipe away the past with a promise of the future. But he only gazed at her and said calmly, slowly, "This is me, remember? I'll be whatever you want me to be."

But she could only deny what she had sensed and what she had seen in his face. "It's just that you're still so grateful for—"

"You're insulting me," he said, cutting her off. "You're saying I don't know the difference between love and gratitude."

"Then you just feel sorry for me. That's it. I've depended on you too much. I've turned to you too many times. And you can't resist helping someone."

"Now you're saying I don't know the difference between love and pity."

"I'm sorry. Of course you do." She searched his tender expression. "But how? When?"

"It just happened. Little by little, I guess. Maybe from the moment I opened my eyes in your bedroom."

"You're my special friend."

"And that's all I'll be. I can't help how I feel, but I can handle it."

They went back to the couch. She relaxed a little.

"I'm sorry," she said again. "I almost wish I...I mean—"

"I think I know what you're trying to say. Once you've had filet mignon, peanut butter just won't do."

"How can you make jokes?"

"I'm not joking. Look, Lisa, it's all right. I told you I can handle it. I have for a long time you know."

Distressed and still slightly shocked, Lisa said, "You know I love you. You're my dearest friend. I love you with all my heart that way."

"I know you do. And I've accepted that. And as far as I'm concerned, nothing's changed."

But sadness darkened her features.

"Forget it," he said sweetly. "Jeffery asked me to take

care of you, and that's exactly what I'm going to do."

"Jeffery asked you to take care of me?"

"I told you he called me before he left."

"Oh, Brian, I'm so sorry."

"He did me a favor, actually."

"No, this is all terribly unfair to you."

"I'm not complaining."

She shook her golden curls. "I've taken advantage of you. But I didn't know. Oh, Brian, you don't really—"

His dark gaze beheld her in loving awareness. "Yes, honey, I do. For all time. But it's all right." He came slowly to his feet. "If you think you can get through the rest of the night, I'm going home and clean this egg off my face."

She rose beside him. "Brian—"

"Hush." He touched a finger gently to her lips and flashed his radiant smile.

"You'll always have that," she said. "It's so special. It always warms my heart."

"I'm glad—I think."

At the door she said, "Brian, I...I mean...Oh, I don't know what—"

"Don't get upset about this," he told her sternly. "I told you, everything's going to be all right."

She smiled and touched his arm. "Why did God make only one person like you?"

✿   ✿   ✿

On the Fourth of July Lisa made the first of several cross-country solo flights, and after much hard work she passed the examination for her commercial license with a single-engine rating. Shortly after that she took the Flight Instrument Rating Test and from there she went on to get a rating in multi-engines. In October she made her first short flight for Southern Pacific Airways. She was thankful for her employer's immediate confidence in her and was eager to prove her merit. But the knowledge of the tremendous responsibility she carried being at the controls of a passenger plane was enough to give her cold chills at first, and she was secretly grateful to occupy the comfortable chair at her desk and let the men do most of the flying.

When Brian resumed his travels, Lisa missed his company on her days off, but he called her when he was out of town, and for the most part their relationship went on as it had in the past. She visited his home and they often went out together. But now that Lisa was aware of his deep feelings for her, she didn't want to do anything that would hurt him. And so she refrained from crying on his shoulder anymore and she consciously avoided any talk about Jeffery.

As the fall of the year gave way to the holiday season, Lisa settled into a new way of life. Both aspects of her job filled many hours now, and she spent her free time in Brian's company whenever possible. As time wore on she began to miss him in a different way when he was out of town. The sound of his voice over the phone, the unexpected sight of him in the doorway, sent waves of excitement through her heart. What was happening to her, she often wondered. She couldn't help being pleased that Brian was in love with her. Pleased? She was overwhelmed! And her affection for him went so deep that she couldn't bear to know she caused him any unhappiness. Yet she realized that this was exactly what she did, although he never let it show. But to think she could ever return his love was a strange notion to her.

Although Lisa was adjusting well to life without Jeffery, and though the separation had ceased to be so painful, she had a strong sense of not being completely fulfilled. Some urgency seemed yet to be stirring within her, some longing she could not explain. She had her church work, and that was good, but still there was a gnawing inside, as if God wanted something more of her.

Whenever she spoke of this unfulfillment to Brian, he

would smile in his special way and tell her that she must discover that "more"—the rest of His plan for her life. That alone would give her the satisfaction for which she yearned. Brian didn't tell Lisa that he believed God's plan for her included a partner—a lifetime partner. He had never felt that way himself until after meeting her. And he didn't say that she was the right partner for him. He knew she would have to come to this realization on her own. He believed that God wanted her with him, helping with his work. He had wanted her to see this before he revealed his love for her, but since he had been unable to keep it from showing any longer, he only hoped she would soon begin to return his deep feelings. The love for her held captive so long in his heart seemed almost ready to burst apart inside of him. So intense had his feelings grown that it didn't occur to him that she might never give back his love.

Early on a hot Saturday morning in mid-July, more than a year after Lisa's parting with Jeffery, the doorbell summoned her from the kitchen. She left her breakfast on the table and went down the hall to answer it.

It was the new minister of youth from her church. Mike Daniels was a tall, fair-haired young man with a graceful athletic build and a jovial, carefree personality. He had a strong spiritual side to his nature that caused Lisa to respect him deeply and view him as an ideal and qualified leader for young people. Almost from their first meeting he had shown a keen interest in her. They had gone out several times, and Lisa knew his feelings for her were growing rapidly. And she liked him very much too, but in the few weeks she had known him she realized she wasn't quite keeping pace with his affection for her. Sometimes she wondered why. It seemed she hardly thought of Jeffery since meeting Mike, but Brian had been a part of the reason she had begun dating him. She thought if she found other interests, if she didn't rely on Brian so much, perhaps in time he might get over his love for her and find someone else. And maybe, free of concern for Brian, her caring for Mike would grow. She really did like him.

"Mike, come in."

"I'm sorry to just barge in on you this way," the good-looking young man said as he strode into her living room and took a seat on the couch.

"Have you had breakfast?"

"Yes—thanks."

"How about some coffee?"

"No, I can't stay. We're meeting at the church at 11 to leave for the swim party. I just came by to ask you a big favor."

"Sure, anything I can do."

"I don't need you today. I have plenty of chaperones for swimming. It's about the retreat to the mountains next month. As you know, we'll have about 50 kids going, and I was depending on Jill Rogers to have the Bible study time with the junior high girls each morning. But she called me last night and she won't be able to go with us after all. Her vacation time from her job has been changed and she can't get off to go."

"Oh, I'm sorry."

"She's really disappointed. She loves working with the kids and she was looking forward to the week in the mountains with them. Lisa, I know this isn't giving you much notice, but I can't think of anyone else who might be able to take her place now. Everybody has vacations all arranged and that kind of thing. Is it possible you could get some time off then?"

She was thoughtful for a minute. "Yes, Mike, I probably could. Vic and Jerry are wonderful to work for. And I haven't planned any vacation time yet." (Didn't want all that time on her hands, Lisa reminded herself.) "If they can manage without me during that week, they'll let me off. It's still more than a month till the retreat. I'll ask them Monday and let you know."

Mike came to his feet, wearing a radiant smile. "I'll be eternally grateful if you can work this out. You can stay with Jill's cabin of girls too." His smile vanished and he gazed tenderly, seriously into her upturned face. "I'll have my hands full with a cabin of boys to stay with and the whole camp to run, but it'll be great just having you around to help out."

"I'll love every minute of it."

"I'll get Jill's Bible study material to you as soon as you let me know if you'll be able to go."

Lisa walked out to the porch with Mike to say good-bye. He bent and kissed her lightly on the cheek just as a silver Imperial swung into the driveway.

"You're getting company," he said, looking up.

Lisa followed his gaze. "It's just Brian Sommervale."

Mike laughed. "Just Brian Sommervale. Imagine taking a guy like that for granted! Do you object if I stay and meet him? It would be an honor just to shake hands with the man."

"The honor will be his, Mike, believe me. That's the way he is."

Chapter 17 ❋❋❋❋❋❋❋❋❋❋

*I*f Brian was honored to meet the handsome young minister of youth from Lisa's church, his feelings of regard vanished rapidly after Mike had taken his leave. When he came back from moving his car to let Mike out of the driveway, he stalked around Lisa's cottage like a caged lion—a caged, *angry*, lion.

He doesn't like it that Mike was here, Lisa told herself, and she couldn't help smiling when, after several attempts at casual conversation, Brian brought up the subject of her new friend. But he brought it up as only Brian Sommervale would.

"Why don't you pack a bag? You won't be coming back till tomorrow night."

"Oh? And where am I going?"

"To my place."

Lisa giggled. The caveman dragging his woman off to his den. But she wasn't Brian's woman.

"How did you know I didn't have to work today?"

"Questions! Questions! What makes a woman so consistently inquisitive?"

Oh, such a mood, thought Lisa.

"How did you know?"

"I'm psychic."

"You're crazy."

Brian had been pacing up and down the living room. Now

he came and took a seat beside Lisa on the couch. He faced her, a look of gloom in his eyes that she hadn't noticed before.

"I'm probably that to."

"Why didn't you just call if you wanted me to come over? Like you usually do."

"I just thought I'd come by for you. It's a good thing I did."

So he'd seen Mike's affectionate kiss.

"Is Mike Daniels a new boyfriend?"

"Well...sort of."

The look of pain in Brian's eyes tore at her heart. Why hadn't she just said no? He really wasn't a boyfriend. Not yet.

In a moment Brian said, "Everybody needs someone. I want you to be happy."

"You need someone too. And I want you to be just as happy."

"I have my work, and since I can't have the woman I want, I'll just drown myself in that."

"That's no excuse. You were drowning yourself in your work when we met."

"I was drowning anyway."

"You *are* crazy," she laughed.

"I'm crazy about *you,*" he said, but ended it there. Though his thoughts formed into many further words, he couldn't say them. How could he tell her that if he lost her again it would be more than he could bear?

"Are you going to get some clothes together for the weekend, or shall I do it for you?"

"Just who do you think you are," she flared, "coming in here and ordering me around? Suppose I don't want to spend the weekend at your place?"

"Are you talking back to me, young lady?" His features were stern, but his tone was teasing.

"So what if I am? Who are you?"

Brian's all-consuming laughter filled the room. His broad shoulders shook riotously. But Lisa felt fury coming alive in her. Sometimes Brian could be acutely overbearing. She gave him a look of utter disgust. "Some Christian gentleman you've turned out to be."

"Do you have a date with Mike Daniels tonight?"

She stared at him from behind an incredulous expression. "You know something? I believe you're just a little too bossy for my taste. And nosy."

Anger clouded Brian's dark eyes. That quick temper he had once warned her about, Lisa thought, but she refused to heed the danger signal. "You think you can just go around telling everybody what to do. I think you've had a part in predicting so many outcomes that it's damaged your thinking!"

Brian gripped her by each arm. "My thinking may be damaged, but not where you're concerned!"

"Where I'm concerned doesn't really concern you!"

Why was she doing this? Did she think she could make him stop caring for her?

"Oh, yes it does!"

"And just what gives you the right? Because you're Brian Sommervale? The *great* Brian So—"

"The way I feel about you gives me the right."

It was the way he said it that touched her—so tenderly, so obviously prompted by strong emotion. Just as suddenly as Lisa's anger had sprung up, it subsided and she was sorry for what she had said.

"Brian—"

"Are you talking back to me again?"

"Yes! Yes!" she almost shouted. And it was fun. Even fighting with Brian was fun.

"I'm sorry I lost my temper," he said, still holding her by the arms.

"I'm sorry too. I don't know what got into me. I love you for being such a wonderful friend. I don't know what I'd ever do without you."

"Say that again."

"I don't know what I'd—"

"No. The first part."

"I said, I love you—"

"That's enough," he said, and touched his lips gently, briefly to hers.

She smiled her wide, even smile. "You tricked me."

"Do you have a date with Mike Daniels tonight?"

"No."

He smiled and slid his arms around her, and for a tender moment they clung to each other. In peace. In harmony. In affection. And Brian marveled at how right it felt to hold her against him. This is where she belongs, he thought. And he couldn't be satisfied until she thought it too.

The weekend at Brian's estate was one of unusual joy for Lisa. She and Brian went with Eric to the beach, where they built castles in the sand and romped blissfully in the surf. They went swimming in the ocean beneath the glistening sun and rode horseback over the shaded grounds. Sunday after church service she enjoyed one of Livy's scrumptuous dinners and played games of chess and ping-pong in the game room.

When Brian brought Lisa home late Sunday night, he kissed her good night at the door. But this kiss was hardly just an affectionate expression from a good friend. Just the thought of it in the days that followed made her heart turn crazy somersaults.

❀   ❀   ❀

A call came from Mike shortly after Lisa got home from work Monday evening.

"Did you work it out with your bosses to get some time off for the retreat?"

"Yes. Everything's all set. Jerry's wife is going to fill in for me."

"That's great. I'll bring the Bible study material over tomorrow night. If you aren't doing anything, maybe we can go out.''

''That'll be fine.''

''I missed you at church yesterday.''

''I went to church with Brian.''

''What is there between you two, anyway? I get a feeling it's more than friendship.''

''Don't be silly. Of course we're just friends.''

At least she was Brian's friend, but he had been so much more to her. And his feelings were stronger than hers too. She thought about the way he had tricked her into saying ''I love you'' and about the passionate kiss he had given her Sunday night. Her precious Brian, the most treasured friend she had in all the world. He was in love with her, but she...she couldn't possibly feel that way about him. Could she?

The following Friday Brian called Lisa and asked her to join him for dinner at his estate. Afterward they went for a walk along the quiet beach. It was a warm, overcast evening, with just a slight breeze stirring the palms and only a gentle surf sweeping across the sand. They hadn't walked very far when Lisa sensed that Brian had something on his mind.

''Do you ever hear from your parents?'' he asked.

''They write often, as I do.''

''How long has it been since you've seen them?''

''You know how long it's been. Since...Thanksgiving Day two years ago.''

''It'll soon be three years then.''

''Yes.''

''Why don't you fly to Amarillo some weekend and see them?''

''You know why—because I can't tell them about Jeffery. I just told them we had stopped seeing each other. But if I go home, I know my mother will ask questions.''

He stopped walking and she drew up beside him. ''I know

I'm interfering where I probably shouldn't, honey, but—''

"Then don't interfere—for once in your life."

"You know I'm not made that way. I can't help interfering when I see a real need."

"I can't go, Brian, I just can't."

"You can. And you will."

"Oh, stop it! You just can't run everybody's life."

"Just yours."

"Not even mine."

"Do you want to go home?"

Her wistful expression told him all he needed to know. "I'd take you myself, but I really feel this is something you need to do alone."

"Then leave me alone and I'll do it...someday."

"Why not this weekend?"

"I have to work tomorrow. Carl and Jerry are both busy. I have to make a short trip."

"Next weekend then."

"I can't."

"Why not?"

"Brian, please—"

The kindness in his handsome face turned to disappointment. "What you mean is you won't."

"No, I can't."

"They'll understand. Throw a few things in a suitcase. File a flight plan and you're off. Where's your flight tomorrow?"

"Just over to Las Vegas. I'm flying a honeymoon couple over."

"I'll make the trip for you."

She set incredulous eyes on him. "You can't do that!"

"Why not? I've got a plane. Insurance. I'm even a good pilot."

"But that's ridiculous. Brian Sommervale flying—"

"Brian Sommervale can do anything he wants to, young lady."

She grinned at him. "You're spoiled. You always get your way. That's what's wrong with you."

"No, honey. I don't always get my way. But I will about this."

"What makes you so sure?" she asked, an impetuous gleam in her bright eyes.

"Because you want to go. You need to go. You owe it to yourself and your parents."

"Oh, Brian, I know you're right, only...I paraded Jeffery before my family as my future husband. I even told my mother I thought we would get engaged that Christmas. Don't you realize how hard it will be to tell her the truth? That I fell in love with a married man? She'll want to know what really went wrong."

"The kind of mother who raised you will respect your privacy if you don't want to talk about it. But you do. You need to, really. And I won't take no for an answer. I'll take you myself next weekend if that's the only way I can get you to go."

This man was unbelievable! And there was no use fighting him. He was right: She ached to see her family again. To know that they understood her mistake with Jeffery, that she hadn't known he was married when she fell in love with him, meant more to her than anything in the world.

❋ ❋ ❋

Brian met Lisa at the airfield when she returned from Amarillo. The glow of renewed radiance on her lovely face told him all he needed to know before she ever spoke a word.

"I should have gone home a long time ago!" she exclaimed as he gave her a hand down from the plane. "I'm glad you insisted. I wouldn't have gone if you hadn't. They were so wonderful. They didn't waste any time in showering me with their love and understanding."

❋ ❋ ❋

The telephone clattered loudly, disturbing the calmness in the dark room. Brian reached over the side of the bed to silence the offending shrill. "Hello," he mumbled into the receiver.

The luminous clock on the night table read four o'clock. Brian jumped up, discarding his pajamas and pulling on a pair of white trousers draped over a nearby chair. He didn't bother to turn on the light, but reached for his glasses on the table and left the room. In the hall he flipped a light switch and hurried along in his bare feet to Lisa's door. His glasses still in one hand, he knocked softly with the other. He waited, and when no response came he knocked louder. She must be sound asleep, he thought, and opened the door quietly and entered the room, his feet soundless on the thick carpet. At the canopy bed he gazed down at her in the pale moonlight streaming through the parted drapes at the French doors. She was a picture of loveliness asleep beneath the pink covers, one hand resting at an angle beside her head of golden hair. But he had no time to think of his beautiful Lisa now or how much he loved her. He was too much distressed.

Leaning over the bed, he shook her gently. She awoke with a start, her lovely green eyes wide with fear at the first sight of him. But it took her only a moment to realize that the man bending so near was her precious Brian. She smiled up sweetly at him, wondering what it was about him that was different. It wasn't just that he was half-dressed, in trousers only, with his broad, tan chest bare before her. It was his face. And she was reminded of the night when she had pulled his weakened body out of the ocean and had then cared for him in the two days and nights that followed. She had decided then that he was about the best-looking man she had ever seen. That was until she had met Jeffery.

"Lisa."

At the sound of his voice it came to her that something must be very wrong. Brian looked so strained, and why had he come to her room and wakened her at what must be quite an early hour?

"I just got a call from the hospital," he said, and sank down on the bed beside her. "Heather's had an accident."

"Oh, no!" She sat up, suddenly alert and concerned. She pulled the cover up around her gown. "How serious is it?"

"They don't know yet. She's just been brought in. Will you go to the hospital with me?"

"Of course I will," she said, holding the cover with one hand and reaching up with the other to brush a lock of dark, shining hair from his forehead. Such a tenderness for Brian consumed her all of a sudden. Brian looked anything but the forceful man that he was, empowered by strength from above. He really does need someone, she thought. He needs the right woman to share his demanding life, to make it complete. Well, he had Maude. And that was good. But he didn't love Maude.

He took Lisa's hand in his own and placed his soft lips upon it. "Hurry and get dressed," he said, rising.

He had started for the door when she called out to him. Smiling almost maternally, she said, "Don't forget to put on your glasses."

In less than an hour Lisa and Brian came through the emergency entrance of the local hospital. At the nurse's station Brian spoke to the acquaintance who had telephoned him about Heather's accident. She was a plain young woman with a long, pointed nose and wispy strands of brown hair.

"Any word yet?" When she shook her head and looked forlornly at him, he said, "Have you found out what happened?"

"The paramedics who brought her in told me her car apparently skidded out of control. They said she was evidently going at a high speed, from the looks of the tire marks on the road. They think she lost control going around a curve."

"Was anyone with her?"

"No. The officers said someone came along seconds after she left the road and came to a stop. Her car had turned over on its side and the people said the wheels were still spinning when they came to the accident. They called the police from the nearest house."

"Did the paramedics say if she was conscious or how bad she appeared to be hurt?"

"I just overheard them say she was bleeding profusely."

Brian glanced around. "I wish someone would come and tell us something," he said gravely.

"Why don't you have a seat, Mr. Sommervale, and I'll see what I can find out." The nurse left her station and went the short distance to the emergency room. She disappeared through the big double doors.

Lisa and Brian crossed the hospital corridor and sat down on a bench along the wall. She reached over and took his hand, giving it a tender squeeze. Neither of them spoke, but his gratitude for her presence was clearly visible in the expression behind the tinted lenses that covered his eyes. They sat there like that, hand in hand, in the clinical atmosphere of the hospital and waited. All around them the sights and sounds of the hospital went on—a voice over the intercom, the clatter of high heels on the polished corridor, a cart being pushed along by a white-clad attendant. But Brian could only think of Heather and whether he would ever see her alive again. For all the power and influence that God had allowed him to have in the world, he had never been able to help his sister. And all he could do now was sit there, clinging to Lisa's hand and praying silently.

Presently the nurse came back accompanied by a short, thickset man in a long white coat. He was about 40 years of age and had the look of someone who had recently been through a long, devastating crisis. Yet he presented an air of peacefulness.

"I'm Dr. Leslie, Mr. Sommervale," the man said as Lisa and Brian came to their feet.

Brian shook his hand. "How do you do, sir?" Then he introduced Lisa to the doctor.

"Mr. Sommervale, I think your sister is going to be all right." A deep sigh of relief escaped between Brian's teeth as the physician went on. "She has some internal injuries, some arteries were damaged, and she has several broken ribs. But we finally got the bleeding stopped, which is what had us most concerned. She's lost a lot of blood, and she'll need time for rest and healing, but barring any complications I don't think you have anything to worry about."

"Thank you very much for all you've done, doctor," Brian said. "When can I see my sister?"

"I think you can see her now, but only for a few minutes."

Heather lay motionless in the bed, her face nearly as white as the blanket that covered her. An intravenous bottle of fluids hung from a metal stand and ran from a tube into her left arm.

When Brian walked over to the bed she opened her dark eyes. "Hello, honey." He bent and kissed her forehead.

She gave him a faint grin. "I didn't think I'd ever see you again."

"You thought that once before, but you were wrong then too." Thanks to Lisa, he thought.

"I've really messed up, haven't I?"

"We'll talk later. You need to rest now. I called Mom and Dad. They're on their way."

She reached out to him and he took her hand. "I'm sorry for all the hurt I've caused you," she said softly. "I didn't mean it."

"I know."

"From now on things are going to be different."

"I'd better go now so you can get some sleep. I'll come back tonight."

"Will you bring Lisa with you?"

"She's with me now."

"I'm glad. But I think I owe her an apology for the way I've treated her."

"She'll be happy to know how you really feel."

"Has she come to her senses yet and realized she's in love with you?"

Brian's face broke into a surprised grin. "Not yet."

Chapter 18 ✷✷✷✷✷✷✷✷✷✷

*L*isa sat on a wooden bench beneath a giant pine tree in a clearing not far from the camp's dining hall and recreation room. She leaned against the bark of the tree gazing dreamily out at the splendid greenery of the wide plateau and high mountain peaks in the distance. The sky was a deep blue, and all around her trees were alive with fresh blossoms and birds sang their cheery tunes. It was the last evening of their week-long retreat with the church youth group. In this natural surrounding, so unadorned with worldly pleasures and temptation, the hearts of the young people had been filled with the joyous Spirit of God and had drawn closer to His love. Some had made their first commitment to Him.

The sound of footfalls crunching on the pine needles strewn thickly on a nearby path brought Lisa out of her reverie. She glanced up to see Mike emerging from the woods. He smiled when he saw her and came to take a seat beside her on the bench.

"It's been quite a week, hasn't it?"

"It's been wonderful," she said. "Everyone's had such a great time, and the kids have grown so much spiritually."

"I don't know about you, but I'm worn out."

"We all are, I think. But it's such a good feeling to be used up in this way."

"I'm sorry I haven't been able to spend any time with you this week."

"Oh, that's all right. This week was for the kids."

Abruptly Mike stood up and reached for her hand. "We don't have much time before supper and the program tonight, but come with me for a walk."

Lisa rose, smiling, and hand in hand they started along the narrow wooded path that led away from the clearing and deep into the forest. The sheltered trail took them along a mountain stream and finally brought them out at the edge of a cliff. They stood overlooking a vast green valley, watching the sunset paint the horizon with a blaze of color. A refreshing breeze rippled among the trees, and the setting sun filled the Western sky with streaks of orange and red and gold.

"Such indescribable beauty," Lisa uttered.

Mike smiled and pulled her to him. The mountian air was growing cooler now, and he held her close, shielding her body from the breeze. Then he bent toward her, his blue eyes tender and laughing, and touched her lips with a gentle kiss. She felt the warmth and powerfulness of this athletic body as he held her, and the sweetness of his kiss enticed her to respond. But momentarily she drew away, a voice inside crying an emphatic no.

Just then a noise in the underbrush nearby startled them, and they looked up to see a tiny fawn scamper out from among a stand of trees. The frightened animal stood rigid, peering keenly at them from clear, dark eyes. Then, as quickly as it had come, the fawn turned back and was lost among the thicket.

The appearance of the small deer had served to break the spell of Mike's kiss, and Lisa could think clearly once more— for all the good that would do her, she thought. She liked Mike—she found him extremely attractive and she had boundless admiration for his work with the young people of their church; she even thought their relationship was headed for growth. But this week it seemed that something inside her said it was not to be. She sensed that Mike was beginning to care for her more and more, but she knew as well that to perpetuate any serious relationship with him would be a gross injustice.

"Lisa, maybe this isn't the time or the place. Or maybe it is. It's the right setting anyway, even if we don't have a lot of time to talk, but—"

"Wait a minute, Mike. Before you say anything more."

Lisa gazed out at the vista of sky and mountains. The brilliant horizon had paled now, the sun filtering slowly down through the rustling trees to disappear from view behind the distant hills.

"I'm sorry if I've...if I've given you false encouragement," she finally said.

"I don't understand."

She faced him slowly. "I like you very much, Mike, but I don't think I can go out with you anymore."

In the faint light from the sky she could see the question in his eyes and the hope mingled there with silent expectation. "Will you tell me why?"

He deserved an answer to that, so why couldn't she give him one?

"Is there someone else?"

Was there? Certainly not Jeffery. Not now. And Brian was only a friend. Her dearest one, but a friend just the same.

In the absence of her comment, Mike went on. "I don't have any right to ask you this, and you don't have to answer if you don't want to, but...are you in love with Brian Sommervale?"

Lisa turned and walked a short distance away. Why did she feel so uneasy all of a sudden?

"I guess I have my answer," he said when she just stood there turned away from him.

"No," she said, still with her back to him, "I'm not in

love with Brian, not in the way you mean."

"I can see now it was foolish to hope it might be me, but you're obviously in love with someone."

She half-turned. "No."

"Not that I know all that much about it, but if you're not a woman in love, then I've never seen one."

She shook her head.

He joined her on the path. "I saw the way he looked at you that Saturday when I was leaving your house. He's crazy about you. Why don't you join forces with him? He looks tired these days. He's probably working too hard. I wonder if he could use a good co-pilot?"

When they emerged from the wooded path, Lisa stepped into the clearing and froze in speechless amazement. Mike glanced across the clearing, then back at her. He smiled and strode toward the wooden bench beneath the giant pine. Brian rose and came to greet him.

The young minister shook hands with him and said, "You're one fortunate man, my friend."

Mike walked away then and left Brian staring after him, an enigmatic expression on his bronze features.

Lisa had recovered from the shock of seeing the philanthropist by this time and went over to the bench, her heart taking strange, giddy leaps in her chest. For goodness sake, what *was* the matter with her?

How sweet and young she looked, Brian thought as she approached. In casual jeans and loose shirt, she seemed like a little girl to him. He resisted a strong urge to scoop her up in his arms.

"What was all that about?"

She flushed beneath her suntan, but decided to ignore his question, especially since she had a more important one of her own to ask. "What are you doing here?"

"Is that a hint of welcome in your voice?"

"You know you're welcome," she said, laughing at him.

"But not for long—is that it?"

He was in another one of those moods, thought Lisa. Was it because he had found her with Mike?

"Don't be silly. Can you stay the night? We're leaving first thing in the morning, but tonight's the Grand Finale Program. There'll be lots of singing and skits and testimonies. You'll stay, won't you ?"

"If I stay around here that long I might do something foolish."

"Like what?"

"Like push Mike over one of these cliffs."

"Oh, Brian, be serious will you?"

"I am, honey, I am." He took her by the hand and led her over to the bench. "Sit down and talk to me," he said. "I came all the way up here to see you, so the least you can do is talk to me."

"Such a long trip," she teased.

"I've been home all week. I missed you."

She had missed him too this week. Strange. He was gone so much—why had he been on her mind more this week than any other?

"What have you been up to all week?" she asked. "I know you haven't been idle."

"Oh, you know me, I've been taking care of business as usual."

"Like what?"

"We've been engaged in a project to distribute books to children who don't have access to any kind of reading material."

"That's so important. We need to educate the world's children, because they're the adults of tomorrow."

Brian's wonderful laughter rang out in the cool night. "Now where did you come up with that piece of brilliance?"

She grinned playfully at him. "Oh, I don't know. I probably heard you say it."

After that neither of them spoke for awhile. Then at last Brian's rich baritone broke the silent spell. "It's really nice up here, isn't it?"

"It's beautiful and peaceful. Like a refuge."

A sudden rustle of leaves in a nearby tree caught Brian's attention. "Hey, look up there!"

She followed his gaze in the near darkness.

"Look up there on that branch. See them?"

She nodded, smiling and watching the two gray squirrels chattering and scampering across a narrow limb. They ran down the trunk in a minute and vanished into a thicket.

"Lisa, let's talk about Mike," Brian said, running one hand absently through his hair.

Was that why he had come up here? Because Mike had been here all week with her? But they had scarcely had time to talk to each other—until this evening. But Brian didn't know that.

"There's nothing to talk about."

"He likes you—a lot."

"I like him—a lot."

"It's time you found someone again."

"Are you trying to fix me up?"

"You know better than that."

"Mike just asked me if I was in love with you."

Brian looked surprised. "What did you tell him?"

She turned away. "I told him...not exactly...I mean... that is..."

"You're making about as much sense as the chattering of those squirrels." He couldn't help smiling. Dare he hope that Lisa was finally...

But instead he said, "Maybe Mike could make you happy."

"Mike will make someone very happy."

"Why not you?"

She fastened her emerald gaze on him. "You said you weren't trying to fix me up."

"Well, why not?"

She shrugged. "How should I know?"

"I'm not trying to fix you up," he said with a smile he could not hide. "I'd be crazy to do a thing like that."

She looked like she was going to laugh.

"I mean really crazy."

"You're still trying to fix me up."

"Never. But I love you enough to want you to be happy, even if that means...someone else."

So taken was she by the truth and sincerity of his words that it was a moment before she could speak. "That's the first time you've ever said that you..."

"I've wanted to tell you so many times."

There was a long silence in which they just looked at each other, deeply, tenderly, earnestly. Then he moved closer to her, taking her face in his hands. "I love you, my darling. You belong with me. And like the old Chinese proverb says, I've belonged to you since the day you saved my life." He kissed her softly, tenderly, lovingly on the mouth, and she slid her arms around his neck, responding to him with all her heart.

❀ ❀ ❀

Brian had been gone for six days. He looked completely exhausted when Lisa met him at the airport the following Saturday night. They spent a relaxing Sunday at his estate, and then early Monday morning he was off again.

"He'll kill himself if he keeps up this pace," she told herself on the way to work later that same morning. Foolish man, she thought. Why doesn't he slow down? He can't solve the world's problems all on his own.

But it soon became apparent to Lisa that he would continue to try. When he called the next Friday and said it would be another week before he returned to Brenthall, she felt like screaming into the telephone receiver. Instead, she wished him all the best, asked God to keep him safe, and spent a miserable week at her own job. It seemed that every waking moment she thought about Brian off in his Lear jet, alone, tired, and perhaps thinking about her. It was almost as if he were trying to run away from something, she thought, or run it down.

Lisa took a flight up to San Francisco the following Saturday. All the way up and back she could only think of Brian and that he was home for a few days of rest. No sooner had she set the plane down on the runway at Southern Pacific Airways than she made up her mind what she must do. But she still didn't know why.

Driving to Brian's estate, she pondered the strange urging that had suddenly overtaken her. She really didn't understand why she was consumed with such a desire to see Brian. He had only been away two weeks, and that wasn't unusual. But she had to see him before he decided to go off somewhere again. Maybe she would even go on his next trip with him, if Vic and Jerry would give her some more time off. She could help with the flying. But that's what he had been wanting! She hadn't wanted it before, but now...

Peter greeted Lisa at the broad front doors, his dark eyes big and round with surprise.

"Oh, Peter, where's Brian? He *is* home, isn't he?"

"Yes, Lisa, He's—"

She didn't wait for the rest of his answer, but ran past the butler, calling over her shoulder, "Never mind, I'll find him."

Peter shook his head as she disappeared down the hall. "I've never seen Lisa in such a hurry."

"If you're not a woman in love I've never seen one," Mike had said.

Well, if she was a woman in love, why didn't she know it? In the next instant she did.

She hastened through the recreation room and came to a stop in the open doorway. Brian was out on the patio standing by the pool. When he turned and saw her, joy lighted his handsome face. He started across the patio and she ran straight to him.

"I don't exactly know what I'm doing here," she began.

He took one look at the glow on her face and the shine in her eyes and smiled triumphantly. "I think I do," he said, and took her in his arms.

She gazed at him with that adoring expression a woman can only have for the man who has claimed the deepest love in her heart. "I've always been in love with you, haven't I?" she softly said.

"Not always."

"I've loved you in one way or another."

"All that matters is the way you love me now."

"My heart had always belonged to you. I was just too blind to see it."

He kissed her tenderly at first, then with a passion that shook her very soul, and she responded with every part of her being.

Later, in the living room, Brian confronted Lisa with some news she didn't expect. "I'm going to be needing a secretary," he said from his place beside her on the couch. "Maude is leaving. She's going to marry her Mexican friend who was here for Christmas."

Lisa fixed an uncertain gaze on him "Why didn't you tell me that before?"

"I wanted you to come to me because you wanted to, not because you thought I needed someone." Before she knew it he had wrapped her in his arms. He held her so tightly that she scarcely had space to breathe. "I wasn't trying to deceive you, honey. It's just that I've loved you so much for so long. I had to be sure this was your choice too, and not just mine."

And it had been the right choice, thought Lisa. They would have a wonderful life. Brian had been given a capacity for love beyond a woman's wildest dreams. To be the object of such a love, to serve the Lord with such a man, was the richest blessing He could bestow.

"But I do know you need someone," she said. "Every man needs to be with the woman he loves. And you're in such a pathetic need of a co-pilot."

He smiled his crooked smile. "I told you we'd make a great team."

"I'm not qualified to fly your jet."

"You'll have to get qualified," he said, smiling again.

"Don't do that. I can't think straight when you smile. I never could."

"You're thinking straight, honey, you're thinking straight for the first time in your life."

"Why, you!" she flared, trying to free herself from his hold. But he wouldn't let her go. She collapsed willingly in his arms. His male strength was too much for her. "I don't know if I'm going to like having you for a boss."

"I don't want to be your boss. I just want to be your husband."

"But you'll be a bossy husband."

"And you'll be a sassy wife. Always talking back."

"But—"

He kissed her before she could protest further. "You're supposed to submit to me, woman."

"And you're supposed to love me as Christ loves the church."

"I'll try my best, sweetheart," he said, gazing into her eyes with a tenderness she would not have believed possible.

"Oh, Brian," was all she could say, so caught up was she in the joy of submitting to that kind of love.

❋   ❋   ❋

Lisa gave Vic and Jerry two weeks' notice, and on the eve of her last day with them Brian and she had dinner at his estate. Later they were on the veranda off the living room when he took her in his arms for a kiss. In a moment she drew away, looking past him to the open doorway.

"What's the matter?"

"What if someone sees us? What if Peter comes out here?"

"So? Holding you in my arms is a sight Peter hasn't seen much, but he'll get used to it. So will everybody else around here."

"Do you think we should be so open with our affections in front of everyone?"

"You aren't going to be that kind of wife, are you?" he asked, still holding her. "No, you aren't going to be that kind of wife!" She smiled at him and he said, "We have some wedding plans to make, honey, as soon as we get back."

"As soon—"

"We leave first thing Monday morning."

"But I'm not packed!"

"You'll learn to get packed quickly," he said with his sweet, crooked smile.

Brian was called to the telephone then, and Lisa decided to go for a walk on the beach. She asked him to join her when he finished.

She left the house by the back door and went through the courtyard and down to the sandy shore. The moon made a full golden circle in the black, starry sky and a breeze blew light and cool as she strolled beside the rushing waves. Ambling along a short distance, she stopped to admire the dark waters of the sea, glistening like silver moonlight. Memory washed over her unexpectedly then, and she thought of Jeffery and the first night he had taken her in his arms there.

"I'll never forget him," she whispered to the breeze, "but this is where my heart belongs."

Brian crossed the rear veranda and made his way down the beach. Soon he caught up to Lisa. She turned from the shimmering ocean as he approached.

"Isn't it the most beautiful sight you've ever seen?"

He gazed out across the silver, gleaming water, then back into her face. "Almost."

They smiled at each other and clasped hands. As they walked along the moonlit shore the only sound to be heard was the murmuring of the waves and the beating of their hearts.